Praise for

we were liars

"**You're going to want to remember the title.** Liars details the summers of a girl who harbors a dark secret, and delivers a satisfying but shocking twist ending." —Breia Brissey, Entertainment Weekly

★"**[A] searing story** . . . At the center of it is a girl who learns the hardest way of all what family means, and what it means to lose the one that really mattered to you." —Publishers Weekly, Starred

★"**Surprising, thrilling, and beautifully executed** in spare, precise, and lyrical prose. Lockhart spins a tragic family drama, the roots of which go back generations. And the ending? Shhhh. Not telling. (But it's a doozy.) . . . This is poised to be big." —Booklist, Starred

"A haunting tale about how families live within their own mythologies. **Sad, wonderful, and real.**" —Scott Westerfeld, author of Uglies and Leviathan

"**Spectacular.**" —Lauren Myracle, author of Shine, The Infinite Moment of Us, and TTYL

"A haunting, brilliant, beautiful book. **This is E. Lockhart at her mind-blowing best.**" —Sarah Mlynowski, author of Don't Even Think About It and Gimme a Call

"Dark, gripping, heartrending, and **terrifyingly smart,** this book grabs you from the first page—and will never let go." —Robin Wasserman, author of The Waking Dark

we were liars

Also by e. lockhart

The Ruby Oliver Novels

The Boyfriend List

The Boy Book

The Treasure Map of Boys

Real Live Boyfriends

. . .

Fly on the Wall

Dramarama

The Disreputable History of Frankie Landau-Banks

How to Be Bad (written with Sarah Mlynowski
and Lauren Myracle)

we were liars

e. lockhart

DELACORTE PRESS

Text copyright © 2014 by E. Lockhart
Jacket photograph © 2014 Getty Images/kang-gg
Map and family tree art copyright © 2014 by Abigail Daker

All rights reserved. Published in the United States by
Delacorte Press, an imprint of Random House Children's Books,
a division of Random House LLC, a Penguin Random House Company, New York.

Delacorte Press is a registered trademark and
the colophon is a trademark of Random House LLC.

Visit us on the Web! randomhouse.com/teens

Educators and librarians, for a variety of teaching tools,
visit us at RHTeachersLibrarians.com

Library of Congress Cataloging-in-Publication Data
We were liars / E. Lockhart. — First edition.
pages cm
Summary: Spending the summers on her family's private island off the coast of
Massachusetts with her cousins and a special boy named Gat, teenaged Cadence
struggles to remember what happened during her fifteenth summer.
ISBN 978-0-385-74126-2 (hardback) — ISBN 978-0-375-98994-0 (library binding) —
ISBN 978-0-375-98440-2 (ebook) — ISBN 978-0-385-39009-5 (intl. tr. pbk.)
[1. Friendship—Fiction. 2. Love—Fiction. 3. Families—Fiction. 4. Amnesia—Fiction.
5. Wealth—Fiction.] I. Title.
PZ7.L79757We 2014
[Fic]—dc23
201342127

The text of this book is set in 12-point Joanna MT.

Book design by Heather Kelly

Printed in the United States of America

10 9 8 7 6

First Edition

For Daniel

Beechwood Island
Massachusetts, USA

Martha's Vineyard Harbor

Staff Dock

Boathouse

Staff Building

Staff Entrance and Mudroom

Perimeter Path

Wooden Walkway

Clairmont
The Sinclairs
Tipper, Harris, and dogs
Prince Philip and Fatima

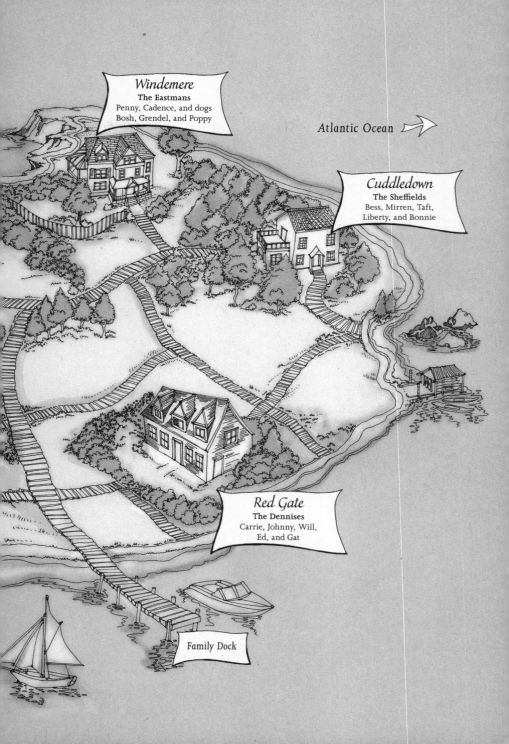

Windemere
The Eastmans
Penny, Cadence, and dogs
Bosh, Grendel, and Poppy

Atlantic Ocean

Cuddledown
The Sheffields
Bess, Mirren, Taft,
Liberty, and Bonnie

Red Gate
The Dennises
Carrie, Johnny, Will,
Ed, and Gat

Family Dock

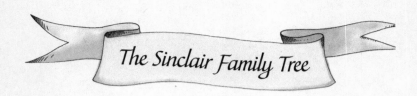

The Sinclair Family Tree

Harris Sinclair & Tipper Taft

Clairmont
and Boston

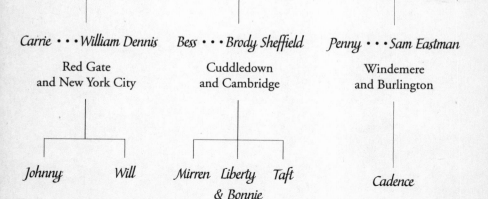

Carrie • • • William Dennis   Bess • • • Brody Sheffield   Penny • • • Sam Eastman

Red Gate   Cuddledown   Windemere
and New York City   and Cambridge   and Burlington

Johnny   Will   Mirren   Liberty   Taft   Cadence
                                        & Bonnie

PART ONE
Welcome

1

WELCOME TO THE beautiful Sinclair family.

No one is a criminal.

No one is an addict.

No one is a failure.

The Sinclairs are athletic, tall, and handsome. We are old-money Democrats. Our smiles are wide, our chins square, and our tennis serves aggressive.

It doesn't matter if divorce shreds the muscles of our hearts so that they will hardly beat without a struggle. It doesn't matter if trust-fund money is running out; if credit card bills go unpaid on the kitchen counter. It doesn't matter if there's a cluster of pill bottles on the bedside table.

It doesn't matter if one of us is desperately, desperately in love.

So much

in love

that equally desperate measures

must be taken.

We are Sinclairs.

No one is needy.

No one is wrong.

We live, at least in the summertime, on a private island off the coast of Massachusetts.

Perhaps that is all you need to know.

2

MY FULL NAME is Cadence Sinclair Eastman.

I live in Burlington, Vermont, with Mummy and three dogs. I am nearly eighteen.

I own a well-used library card and not much else, though it is true I live in a grand house full of expensive, useless objects.

I used to be blond, but now my hair is black.

I used to be strong, but now I am weak.

I used to be pretty, but now I look sick.

It is true I suffer migraines since my accident.

It is true I do not suffer fools.

I like a twist of meaning. You see? *Suffer* migraines. Do not *suffer* fools. The word means almost the same as it did in the previous sentence, but not quite.

Suffer.

You could say it means endure, but that's not exactly right.

MY STORY STARTS before the accident. June of the summer I was fifteen, my father ran off with some woman he loved more than us.

Dad was a middling-successful professor of military history. Back then I adored him. He wore tweed jackets. He was gaunt. He drank milky tea. He was fond of board games and let me win, fond of boats and taught me to kayak, fond of bicycles, books, and art museums.

4

He was never fond of dogs, and it was a sign of how much he loved my mother that he let our golden retrievers sleep on the sofas and walked them three miles every morning. He was never fond of my grandparents, either, and it was a sign of how much he loved both me and Mummy that he spent every summer in Windemere House on Beechwood Island, writing articles on wars fought long ago and putting on a smile for the relatives at every meal.

That June, summer fifteen, Dad announced he was leaving and departed two days later. He told my mother he wasn't a Sinclair, and couldn't try to be one, any longer. He couldn't smile, couldn't lie, couldn't be part of that beautiful family in those beautiful houses.

Couldn't. Couldn't. Wouldn't.

He had hired moving vans already. He'd rented a house, too. My father put a last suitcase into the backseat of the Mercedes (he was leaving Mummy with only the Saab), and started the engine.

Then he pulled out a handgun and shot me in the chest. I was standing on the lawn and I fell. The bullet hole opened wide and my heart rolled out of my rib cage and down into a flower bed. Blood gushed rhythmically from my open wound,

then from my eyes,

my ears,

my mouth.

It tasted like salt and failure. The bright red shame of being unloved soaked the grass in front of our house, the bricks of the path, the steps to the porch. My heart spasmed among the peonies like a trout.

Mummy snapped. She said to get hold of myself.

Be normal, now, she said. Right now, she said.

Because you are. Because you can be.

Don't cause a scene, she told me. Breathe and sit up.

I did what she asked.

She was all I had left.

Mummy and I tilted our square chins high as Dad drove down the hill. Then we went indoors and trashed the gifts he'd given us: jewelry, clothes, books, anything. In the days that followed, we got rid of the couch and armchairs my parents had bought together. Tossed the wedding china, the silver, the photographs.

We purchased new furniture. Hired a decorator. Placed an order for Tiffany silverware. Spent a day walking through art galleries and bought paintings to cover the empty spaces on our walls.

We asked Granddad's lawyers to secure Mummy's assets.

Then we packed our bags and went to Beechwood Island.

3

PENNY, CARRIE, AND Bess are the daughters of Tipper and Harris Sinclair. Harris came into his money at twenty-one after Harvard and grew the fortune doing business I never bothered to understand. He inherited houses and land. He made intelligent decisions about the stock market. He married Tipper and kept her in the kitchen and the garden. He put her on display in pearls and on sailboats. She seemed to enjoy it.

Granddad's only failure was that he never had a son, but no matter. The Sinclair daughters were sunburnt and blessed. Tall, merry, and rich, those girls were like princesses in a fairy tale. They were known throughout Boston, Harvard Yard, and Martha's Vineyard for their cashmere cardigans and grand parties. They were made for legends. Made for princes and Ivy League schools, ivory statues and majestic houses.

Granddad and Tipper loved the girls so, they couldn't say whom they loved best. First Carrie, then Penny, then Bess, then Carrie again. There were splashy weddings with salmon and harpists, then bright blond grandchildren and funny blond dogs. No one could ever have been prouder of their beautiful American girls than Tipper and Harris were, back then.

They built three new houses on their craggy private island and gave them each a name: Windemere for Penny, Red Gate for Carrie, and Cuddledown for Bess.

I am the eldest Sinclair grandchild. Heiress to the island, the fortune, and the expectations.

Well, probably.

4

ME, JOHNNY, MIRREN, and Gat. Gat, Mirren, Johnny, and me.

The family calls us four the Liars, and probably we deserve it. We are all nearly the same age, and we all have birthdays in the fall. Most years on the island, we've been trouble.

Gat started coming to Beechwood the year we were eight. Summer eight, we called it.

Before that, Mirren, Johnny, and I weren't Liars. We were

nothing but cousins, and Johnny was a pain because he didn't like playing with girls.

Johnny, he is bounce, effort, and snark. Back then he would hang our Barbies by the necks or shoot us with guns made of Lego.

Mirren, she is sugar, curiosity, and rain. Back then she spent long afternoons with Taft and the twins, splashing at the big beach, while I drew pictures on graph paper and read in the hammock on the Clairmont house porch.

Then Gat came to spend the summers with us.

Aunt Carrie's husband left her when she was pregnant with Johnny's brother, Will. I don't know what happened. The family never speaks of it. By summer eight, Will was a baby and Carrie had taken up with Ed already.

This Ed, he was an art dealer and he adored the kids. That was all we'd heard about him when Carrie announced she was bringing him to Beechwood, along with Johnny and the baby.

They were the last to arrive that summer, and most of us were on the dock waiting for the boat to pull in. Granddad lifted me up so I could wave at Johnny, who was wearing an orange life vest and shouting over the prow.

Granny Tipper stood next to us. She turned away from the boat for a moment, reached in her pocket, and brought out a white peppermint. Unwrapped it and tucked it into my mouth.

As she looked back at the boat, Gran's face changed. I squinted to see what she saw.

Carrie stepped off with Will on her hip. He was in a baby's yellow life vest, and was really no more than a shock of white-blond hair sticking up over it. A cheer went up at the sight of him. That vest, which we had all worn as babies. The hair. How wonderful that this little boy we didn't know yet was so obviously a Sinclair.

Johnny leapt off the boat and threw his own vest on the dock. First thing, he ran up to Mirren and kicked her. Then he kicked me. Kicked the twins. Walked over to our grandparents and stood up straight. "Good to see you, Granny and Granddad. I look forward to a happy summer."

Tipper hugged him. "Your mother told you to say that, didn't she?"

"Yes," said Johnny. "And I'm to say, nice to see you again."

"Good boy."

"Can I go now?"

Tipper kissed his freckled cheek. "Go on, then."

Ed followed Johnny, having stopped to help the staff unload the luggage from the motorboat. He was tall and slim. His skin was very dark: Indian heritage, we'd later learn. He wore black-framed glasses and was dressed in dapper city clothes: a linen suit and striped shirt. The pants were wrinkled from traveling.

Granddad set me down.

Granny Tipper's mouth made a straight line. Then she showed all her teeth and went forward.

"You must be Ed. What a lovely surprise."

He shook hands. "Didn't Carrie tell you we were coming?"

"Of course she did."

Ed looked around at our white, white family. Turned to Carrie. "Where's Gat?"

They called for him, and he climbed from the inside of the boat, taking off his life vest, looking down to undo the buckles.

"Mother, Dad," said Carrie, "we brought Ed's nephew to play with Johnny. This is Gat Patil."

Granddad reached out and patted Gat's head. "Hello, young man."

"Hello."

"His father passed on, just this year," explained Carrie. "He and Johnny are the best of friends. It's a big help to Ed's sister if we take him for a few weeks. And, Gat? You'll get to have cookouts and go swimming like we talked about. Okay?"

But Gat didn't answer. He was looking at me.

His nose was dramatic, his mouth sweet. Skin deep brown, hair black and waving. Body wired with energy. Gat seemed spring-loaded. Like he was searching for something. He was contemplation and enthusiasm. Ambition and strong coffee. I could have looked at him forever.

Our eyes locked.

I turned and ran away.

Gat followed. I could hear his feet behind me on the wooden walkways that cross the island.

I kept running. He kept following.

Johnny chased Gat. And Mirren chased Johnny.

The adults remained talking on the dock, circling politely around Ed, cooing over baby Will. The littles did whatever littles do.

We four stopped running at the tiny beach down by Cuddledown House. It's a small stretch of sand with high rocks on either side. No one used it much, back then. The big beach had softer sand and less seaweed.

Mirren took off her shoes and the rest of us followed. We tossed stones into the water. We just existed.

I wrote our names in the sand.

Cadence, Mirren, Johnny, and Gat.

Gat, Johnny, Mirren, and Cadence.

That was the beginning of us.

* * *

JOHNNY BEGGED TO have Gat stay longer.

He got what he wanted.

The next year he begged to have him come for the entire summer.

Gat came.

Johnny was the first grandson. My grandparents almost never said no to Johnny.

5

SUMMER FOURTEEN, GAT and I took out the small motorboat alone. It was just after breakfast. Bess made Mirren play tennis with the twins and Taft. Johnny had started running that year and was doing loops around the perimeter path. Gat found me in the Clairmont kitchen and asked, did I want to take the boat out?

"Not really." I wanted to go back to bed with a book.

"Please?" Gat almost never said please.

"Take it out yourself."

"I can't borrow it," he said. "I don't feel right."

"Of course you can borrow it."

"Not without one of you."

He was being ridiculous. "Where do you want to go?" I asked.

"I just want to get off-island. Sometimes I can't stand it here."

I couldn't imagine, then, what it was he couldn't stand, but I said all right. We motored out to sea in wind jackets and bathing suits. After a bit, Gat cut the engine. We sat eating pistachios and breathing salt air. The sunlight shone on the water.

"Let's go in," I said.

Gat jumped and I followed, but the water was so much colder than off the beach, it snatched our breath. The sun went behind a cloud. We laughed panicky laughs and shouted that it was the stupidest idea to get in the water. What had we been thinking? There were sharks off the coast, everybody knew that.

Don't talk about sharks, God! We scrambled and pushed each other, struggling to be the first one up the ladder at the back of the boat.

After a minute, Gat leaned back and let me go first. "Not because you're a girl but because I'm a good person," he told me.

"Thanks." I stuck out my tongue.

"But when a shark bites my legs off, promise to write a speech about how awesome I was."

"Done," I said. "Gatwick Matthew Patil made a delicious meal."

It seemed hysterically funny to be so cold. We didn't have towels. We huddled together under a fleece blanket we found under the seats, our bare shoulders touching each other. Cold feet, on top of one another.

"This is only so we don't get hypothermia," said Gat. "Don't think I find you pretty or anything."

"I know you don't."

"You're hogging the blanket."

"Sorry."

A pause.

Gat said, "I do find you pretty, Cady. I didn't mean that the way it came out. In fact, when did you get so pretty? It's distracting."

"I look the same as always."

"You changed over the school year. It's putting me off my game."

"You have a game?"

He nodded solemnly.

"That is the dumbest thing I ever heard. What is your game?"

"Nothing penetrates my armor. Hadn't you noticed?"

That made me laugh. "No."

"Damn. I thought it was working."

We changed the subject. Talked about bringing the littles to Edgartown to see a movie in the afternoon, about sharks and whether they really ate people, about *Plants Versus Zombies*.

Then we drove back to the island.

Not long after that, Gat started lending me his books and finding me at the tiny beach in the early evenings. He'd search me out when I was lying on the Windemere lawn with the goldens.

We started walking together on the path that circles the island, Gat in front and me behind. We'd talk about books or invent imaginary worlds. Sometimes we'd end up walking several times around the edge before we got hungry or bored.

Beach roses lined the path, deep pink. Their smell was faint and sweet.

One day I looked at Gat, lying in the Clairmont hammock with a book, and he seemed, well, like he was mine. Like he was my particular person.

I got in the hammock next to him, silently. I took the pen

out of his hand—he always read with a pen—and wrote *Gat* on the back of his left, and *Cadence* on the back of his right.

He took the pen from me. Wrote *Gat* on the back of my left, and *Cadence* on the back of my right.

I am not talking about fate. I don't believe in destiny or soul mates or the supernatural. I just mean we understood each other. All the way.

But we were only fourteen. I had never kissed a boy, though I would kiss a few the next school year, and somehow we didn't label it love.

6

SUMMER FIFTEEN I arrived a week later than the others. Dad had left us, and Mummy and I had all that shopping to do, consulting the decorator and everything.

Johnny and Mirren met us at the dock, pink in the cheeks and full of summer plans. They were staging a family tennis tournament and had bookmarked ice cream recipes. We would go sailing, build bonfires.

The littles swarmed and yelled like always. The aunts smiled chilly smiles. After the bustle of arrival, everyone went to Clairmont for cocktail hour.

I went to Red Gate, looking for Gat. Red Gate is a much smaller house than Clairmont, but it still has four bedrooms up top. It's where Johnny, Gat, and Will lived with Aunt Carrie—plus Ed, when he was there, which wasn't often.

I walked to the kitchen door and looked through the screen.

Gat didn't see me at first. He was standing at the counter wearing a worn gray T-shirt and jeans. His shoulders were broader than I remembered.

He untied a dried flower from where it hung upside down on a ribbon in the window over the sink. The flower was a beach rose, pink and loosely constructed, the kind that grows along the Beechwood perimeter.

Gat, my Gat. He had picked me a rose from our favorite walking place. He had hung it to dry and waited for me to arrive on the island so he could give it to me.

I had kissed an unimportant boy or three by now.

I had lost my dad.

I had come here to this island from a house of tears and falsehood

and I saw Gat,

and I saw that rose in his hand,

and in that one moment, with the sunlight from the window shining in on him,

the apples on the kitchen counter,

the smell of wood and ocean in the air,

I did call it love.

It *was* love, and it hit me so hard I leaned against the screen door that still stood between us, just to stay vertical. I wanted to touch him like he was a bunny, a kitten, something so special and soft your fingertips can't leave it alone. The universe was good because he was in it. I loved the hole in his jeans and the dirt on his bare feet and the scab on his elbow and the scar that laced through one eyebrow. Gat, my Gat.

As I stood there, staring, he put the rose in an envelope. He searched for a pen, banging drawers open and shut, found one in his own pocket, and wrote.

I didn't realize he was writing an address until he pulled a roll of stamps from a kitchen drawer.

Gat stamped the envelope. Wrote a return address.

It wasn't for me.

I left the Red Gate door before he saw me and ran down to the perimeter. I watched the darkening sky, alone.

I tore all the roses off a single sad bush and threw them, one after the other, into the angry sea.

7

JOHNNY TOLD ME about the New York girlfriend that evening. Her name was Raquel. Johnny had even met her. He lives in New York, like Gat does, but downtown with Carrie and Ed, while Gat lives uptown with his mom. Johnny said Raquel was a modern dancer and wore black clothes.

Mirren's brother, Taft, told me Raquel had sent Gat a package of homemade brownies. Liberty and Bonnie told me Gat had pictures of her on his phone.

Gat didn't mention her at all, but he had trouble meeting my eyes.

That first night, I cried and bit my fingers and drank wine I snuck from the Clairmont pantry. I spun violently into the sky, raging and banging stars from their moorings, swirling and vomiting.

I hit my fist into the wall of the shower. I washed off the shame and anger in cold, cold water. Then I shivered in my bed like the abandoned dog that I was, my skin shaking over my bones.

The next morning, and every day thereafter, I acted normal. I tilted my square chin high.

We sailed and made bonfires. I won the tennis tournament.

We made vats of ice cream and lay in the sun.

One night, the four of us ate a picnic down on the tiny beach. Steamed clams, potatoes, and sweet corn. The staff made it. I didn't know their names.

Johnny and Mirren carried the food down in metal roasting pans. We ate around the flames of our bonfire, dripping butter onto the sand. Then Gat made triple-decker s'mores for all of us. I looked at his hands in the firelight, sliding marshmallows onto a long stick. Where once he'd had our names written, now he had taken to writing the titles of books he wanted to read.

That night, on the left: *Being and*. On the right: *Nothingness*.

I had writing on my hands, too. A quotation I liked. On the left: *Live in*. On the right: *today*.

"Want to know what I'm thinking about?" Gat asked.

"Yes," I said.

"No," said Johnny.

"I'm wondering how we can say your granddad owns this island. Not legally but actually."

"Please don't get started on the evils of the Pilgrims," moaned Johnny.

"No. I'm asking, how can we say land belongs to *anyone*?" Gat waved at the sand, the ocean, the sky.

Mirren shrugged. "People buy and sell land all the time."

"Can't we talk about sex or murder?" asked Johnny.

Gat ignored him. "Maybe land shouldn't belong to people at all. Or maybe there should be limits on what they can own." He leaned forward. "When I went to India this winter, on that

17

volunteer trip, we were building toilets. Building them because people there, in this one village, didn't *have* them."

"We all know you went to India," said Johnny. "You told us like forty-seven times."

Here is something I love about Gat: he is so enthusiastic, so relentlessly interested in the world, that he has trouble imagining the possibility that other people will be bored by what he's saying. Even when they tell him outright. But also, he doesn't like to let us off easy. He wants to make us think—even when we don't feel like thinking.

He poked a stick into the embers. "I'm saying we should talk about it. Not everyone has private islands. Some people work on them. Some work in factories. Some don't have work. Some don't have food."

"Stop talking, now," said Mirren.

"Stop talking, forever," said Johnny.

"We have a warped view of humanity on Beechwood," Gat said. "I don't think you see that."

"Shut up," I said. "I'll give you more chocolate if you shut up."

And Gat did shut up, but his face contorted. He stood abruptly, picked up a rock from the sand, and threw it with all his force. He pulled off his sweatshirt and kicked off his shoes. Then he walked into the sea in his jeans.

Angry.

I watched the muscles of his shoulders in the moonlight, the spray kicking up as he splashed in. He dove and I thought: If I don't follow him now, that girl Raquel's got him. If I don't follow him now, he'll go away. From the Liars, from the island, from our family, from me.

I threw off my sweater and followed Gat into the sea in my dress. I crashed into the water, swimming out to where he lay on his back. His wet hair was slicked off his face, showing the thin scar through one eyebrow.

I reached for his arm. "Gat."

He startled. Stood in the waist-high sea.

"Sorry," I whispered.

"I don't tell you to shut up, Cady," he said. "I don't ever say that to you."

"I know."

He was silent.

"Please don't shut up," I said.

I felt his eyes go over my body in my wet dress. "I talk too much," he said. "I politicize everything."

"I like it when you talk," I said, because it was true. When I stopped to listen, I did like it.

"It's that everything makes me . . ." He paused. "Things are messed up in the world, that's all."

"Yeah."

"Maybe I should"—Gat took my hands, turned them over to look at the words written on the backs—"I should *live for today* and not be agitating all the time."

My hand was in his wet hand.

I shivered. His arms were bare and wet. We used to hold hands all the time, but he hadn't touched me all summer.

"It's good that you look at the world the way you do," I told him.

Gat let go of me and leaned back into the water. "Johnny wants me to shut up. I'm boring you and Mirren."

I looked at his profile. He wasn't just Gat. He was contemplation and enthusiasm. Ambition and strong coffee. All that was there, in the lids of his brown eyes, his smooth skin, his lower lip pushed out. There was coiled energy inside.

"I'll tell you a secret," I whispered.

"What?"

I reached out and touched his arm again. He didn't pull away. "When we say *Shut up, Gat,* that isn't what we mean at all."

"No?"

"What we mean is, we love you. You remind us that we're selfish bastards. You're not one of us, that way."

He dropped his eyes. Smiled. "Is that what *you* mean, Cady?"

"Yes," I told him. I let my fingers trail down his floating, outstretched arm.

"I can't believe you are in that water!" Johnny was standing ankle-deep in the ocean, his jeans rolled up. "It's the Arctic. My toes are freezing off."

"It's nice once you get in," Gat called back.

"Seriously?"

"Don't be weak!" yelled Gat. "Be manly and get in the stupid water."

Johnny laughed and charged in. Mirren followed.

And it was—exquisite.

The night looming above us. The hum of the ocean. The bark of gulls.

8

THAT NIGHT I had trouble sleeping.

After midnight, he called my name.

I looked out my window. Gat was lying on his back on the wooden walkway that leads to Windemere. The golden retrievers were lying near him, all five: Bosh, Grendel, Poppy, Prince Philip, and Fatima. Their tails thumped gently.

The moonlight made them all look blue.

"Come down," he called.

I did.

Mummy's light was out. The rest of the island was dark. We were alone, except for all the dogs.

"Scoot," I told him. The walkway wasn't wide. When I lay down next to him, our arms touched, mine bare and his in an olive-green hunting jacket.

We looked at the sky. So many stars, it seemed like a celebration, a grand, illicit party the galaxy was holding after the humans had been put to bed.

I was glad Gat didn't try to sound knowledgeable about constellations or say stupid stuff about wishing on stars. But I didn't know what to make of his silence, either.

"Can I hold your hand?" he asked.

I put mine in his.

"The universe is seeming really huge right now," he told me. "I need something to hold on to."

"I'm here."

His thumb rubbed the center of my palm. All my nerves concentrated there, alive to every movement of his skin on mine. "I am not sure I'm a good person," he said after a while.

"I'm not sure I am, either," I said. "I'm winging it."

"Yeah." Gat was silent for a moment. "Do you believe in God?"

"Halfway." I tried to think about it seriously. I knew Gat wouldn't settle for a flippant answer. "When things are bad, I'll pray or imagine someone watching over me, listening. Like the first few days after my dad left, I thought about God. For protection. But the rest of the time, I'm trudging along in my everyday life. It's not even slightly spiritual."

"I don't believe anymore," Gat said. "That trip to India, the poverty. No God I can imagine would let that happen. Then I came home and started noticing it on the streets of New York. People sick and starving in one of the richest nations in the world. I just—I can't think that anyone's watching over those people. Which means no one is watching over me, either."

"That doesn't make you a bad person."

"My mother believes. She was raised Buddhist but goes to Methodist church now. She's not very happy with me." Gat hardly ever talked about his mother.

"You can't believe just because she tells you to," I said.

"No. The question is: how to be a good person if I don't believe anymore."

We stared at the sky. The dogs went into Windemere via the dog flap.

"You're cold," Gat said. "Let me give you my jacket."

I wasn't cold but I sat up. He sat up, too. Unbuttoned his olive hunting jacket and shrugged it off. Handed it to me.

It was warm from his body. Much too wide across the shoulders. His arms were bare now.

I wanted to kiss him there while I was wearing his hunting jacket. But I didn't.

Maybe he loved Raquel. Those photos on his phone. That dried beach rose in an envelope.

9

AT BREAKFAST THE next morning, Mummy asked me to go through Dad's things in the Windemere attic and take what I wanted. She would get rid of the rest.

Windemere is gabled and angular. Two of the five bedrooms have slanted roofs, and it's the only house on the island with a full attic. There's a big porch and a modern kitchen, updated with marble countertops that look a little out of place. The rooms are airy and filled with dogs.

Gat and I climbed up to the attic with glass bottles of iced tea and sat on the floor. The room smelled like wood. A square of light glowed through from the window.

We had been in the attic before.

Also, we had never been in the attic before.

The books were Dad's vacation reading. All sports memoirs, cozy mysteries, and rock star tell-alls by old people I'd never heard of. Gat wasn't really looking. He was sorting the books by color. A red pile, a blue, brown, white, yellow.

"Don't you want anything to read?" I asked.

"Maybe."

"How about *First Base and Way Beyond*?"

Gat laughed. Shook his head. Straightened his blue pile.

"*Rock On with My Bad Self? Hero of the Dance Floor?*"

He was laughing again. Then serious. "Cadence?"

"What?"

"Shut up."

I let myself look at him a long time. Every curve of his face was familiar, and also, I had never seen him before.

Gat smiled. Shining. Bashful. He got to his knees, kicking over his colorful book piles in the process. He reached out and stroked my hair. "I love you, Cady. I mean it."

I leaned in and kissed him.

He touched my face. Ran his hand down my neck and along my collarbone. The light from the attic window shone down on us. Our kiss was electric and soft,

and tentative and certain,

terrifying and exactly right.

I felt the love rush from me to Gat and from Gat to me.

We were warm and shivering,

and young and ancient,

and alive.

I was thinking, It's true. We already love each other.

We already do.

10

GRANDDAD WALKED IN on us. Gat sprang up. Stepped awkwardly on the color-sorted books that had spilled across the floor.

"I am interrupting," Granddad said.

"No, sir."

"Yes, I most certainly am."

"Sorry about the dust," I said. Awkward.

"Penny thought there might be something I'd like to read." Granddad pulled an old wicker chair to the center of the room and sat down, bending over the books.

Gat remained standing. He had to bend his head beneath the attic's slanted roof.

"Watch yourself, young man," said Granddad, sharp and sudden.

"Pardon me?"

"Your head. You could get hurt."

"You're right," said Gat. "You're right, I could get hurt."

"So watch yourself," Granddad repeated.

Gat turned and went down the stairs without another word.

Granddad and I sat in silence for a moment.

"He likes to read," I said eventually. "I thought he might want some of Dad's books."

"You are very dear to me, Cady," said Granddad, patting my shoulder. "My first grandchild."

"I love you, too, Granddad."

"Remember how I took you to a baseball game? You were only four."

"Sure."

"You had never had Cracker Jack," said Granddad.

"I know. You bought two boxes."

"I had to put you on my lap so you could see. You remember that, Cady?"

I did.

"Tell me."

I knew the kind of answer Granddad wanted me to give. It was a request he made quite often. He loved retelling key moments in Sinclair family history, enlarging their importance.

He was always asking what something meant to you, and you were supposed to come back with details. Images. Maybe a lesson learned.

Usually, I adored telling these stories and hearing them told. The legendary Sinclairs, what fun we'd had, how beautiful we were. But that day, I didn't want to.

"It was your first baseball game," Granddad prompted. "Afterward I bought you a red plastic bat. You practiced your swing on the lawn of the Boston house."

Did Granddad know what he'd interrupted? Would he care if he did know?

When would I see Gat again?

Would he break up with Raquel?

What would happen between us?

"You wanted to make Cracker Jack at home," Granddad went on, though he knew I knew the story. "And Penny helped you make it. But you cried when there weren't any red and white boxes to put it in. Do you remember that?"

"Yes, Granddad," I said, giving in. "You went all the way back to the ballpark that same day and bought two more boxes of Cracker Jack. You ate them on the drive home, just so you could give me the boxes. I remember."

Satisfied, he stood up and we left the attic together. Granddad was shaky going downstairs, so he put his hand on my shoulder.

I FOUND GAT on the perimeter path and ran to where he stood, looking out at the water. The wind was coming hard and my hair flew in my eyes. When I kissed him, his lips were salty.

11

GRANNY TIPPER DIED of heart failure eight months before summer fifteen on Beechwood. She was a stunning woman, even when she was old. White hair, pink cheeks; tall and angular. She's the one who made Mummy love dogs so much. She always had at least two and sometimes four golden retrievers when her girls were little, all the way until she died.

She was quick to judge and played favorites, but she was also warm. If you got up early on Beechwood, back when we were small, you could go to Clairmont and wake Gran. She'd have muffin batter sitting in the fridge, and would pour it into tins and let you eat as many warm muffins as you wanted, before the rest of the island woke up. She'd take us berry picking and help us make pie or something she called a slump that we'd eat that night.

One of her charity projects was a benefit party each year for the Farm Institute on Martha's Vineyard. We all used to go. It was outdoors, in beautiful white tents. The littles would run around wearing party clothes and no shoes. Johnny, Mirren, Gat, and I snuck glasses of wine and felt giddy and silly. Gran danced with Johnny and then my dad, then with Granddad, holding the edge of her skirt with one hand. I used to have a photograph of Gran from one of those benefit parties. She wore an evening gown and held a piglet.

Summer fifteen on Beechwood, Granny Tipper was gone. Clairmont felt empty.

The house is a three-story gray Victorian. There is a turret up top and a wraparound porch. Inside, it is full of original *New Yorker* cartoons, family photos, embroidered pillows, small statues, ivory paperweights, taxidermied fish on plaques. Everywhere, everywhere, are beautiful objects collected by Tipper and Granddad. On the lawn is an enormous picnic table, big enough to seat sixteen, and a ways off from that, a tire swing hangs from a massive maple.

Gran used to bustle in the kitchen and plan outings. She made quilts in her craft room, and the hum of the sewing machine could be heard throughout the downstairs. She bossed the groundskeepers in her gardening gloves and blue jeans.

Now the house was quiet. No cookbooks left open on the counter, no classical music on the kitchen sound system. But it was still Gran's favorite soap in all the soap dishes. Those were her plants growing in the garden. Her wooden spoons, her cloth napkins.

One day, when no one else was around, I went into the craft room at the back of the ground floor. I touched Gran's collection of fabrics, the shiny bright buttons, the colored threads.

My head and shoulders melted first, followed by my hips and knees. Before long I was a puddle, soaking into the pretty cotton prints. I drenched the quilt she never finished, rusted the metal parts of her sewing machine. I was pure liquid loss, then, for an hour or two. My grandmother, my grandmother. Gone forever, though I could smell her Chanel perfume on the fabrics.

Mummy found me.

She made me act normal. Because I was. Because I could. She told me to breathe and sit up.

And I did what she asked. Again.

Mummy was worried about Granddad. He was shaky on his feet with Gran gone, holding on to chairs and tables to keep his balance. He was the head of the family. She didn't want him destabilized. She wanted him to know his children and grandchildren were still around him, strong and merry as ever. It was important, she said; it was kind; it was best. Don't cause distress, she said. Don't remind people of a loss. "Do you understand, Cady? Silence is a protective coating over pain."

I understood, and I managed to erase Granny Tipper from conversation, the same way I had erased my father. Not happily, but thoroughly. At meals with the aunts, on the boat with Granddad, even alone with Mummy—I behaved as if those two critical people had never existed. The rest of the Sinclairs did the same. When we were all together, people kept their smiles wide. We had done the same when Bess left Uncle Brody, the same when Uncle William left Carrie, the same when Gran's dog Peppermill died of cancer.

Gat never got it, though. He'd mention my father quite a lot, actually. Dad had found Gat both a decent chess opponent and a willing audience for his boring stories about military history, so they'd spent some time together. "Remember when your father caught that big crab in a bucket?" Gat would say. Or to Mummy: "Last year Sam told me there's a fly-fishing kit in the boathouse; do you know where it is?"

Dinner conversation stopped sharply when he'd mention Gran. Once Gat said, "I miss the way she'd stand at the foot of the table and serve out dessert, don't you? It was so Tipper." Johnny had to start talking loudly about Wimbledon until the dismay faded from our faces.

Every time Gat said these things, so casual and truthful, so oblivious—my veins opened. My wrists split. I bled down my palms. I went light-headed. I'd stagger from the table or collapse in quiet shameful agony, hoping no one in the family would notice. Especially not Mummy.

Gat almost always saw, though. When blood dripped on my bare feet or poured over the book I was reading, he was kind. He wrapped my wrists in soft white gauze and asked me questions about what had happened. He asked about Dad and about Gran—as if talking about something could make it better. As if wounds needed attention.

He was a stranger in our family, even after all those years.

WHEN I WASN'T bleeding, and when Mirren and Johnny were snorkeling or wrangling the littles, or when everyone lay on couches watching movies on the Clairmont flat-screen, Gat and I hid away. We sat on the tire swing at midnight, our arms and legs wrapped around each other, lips warm against cool night skin. In the mornings we'd sneak laughing down to the Clairmont basement, which was lined with wine bottles and encyclopedias. There we kissed and marveled at one another's existence, feeling secret and lucky. Some days he wrote me notes and left them with small presents under my pillow.

> Someone once wrote that a novel should deliver a series of small astonishments. I get the same thing spending an hour with you.
> Also, here is a green toothbrush tied in a ribbon.
> It expresses my feelings inadequately.

> Better than chocolate, being with you last night.
> Silly me, I thought that nothing was better than chocolate.

In a profound, symbolic gesture, I am giving you this bar of
Vosges I got when we all went to Edgartown. You can eat it, or
just sit next to it and feel superior.

I didn't write back, but I drew Gat silly crayon drawings of
the two of us. Stick figures waving from in front of the Colosseum, the Eiffel Tower, on top of a mountain, on the back of a
dragon. He stuck them up over his bed.

He touched me whenever he could. Beneath the table at dinner, in the kitchen the moment it was empty. Covertly, hilari-
ously, behind Granddad's back while he drove the motorboat. I
felt no barrier between us. As long as no one was looking, I ran
my fingers along Gat's cheekbones, down his back. I reached
for his hand, pressed my thumb against his wrist, and felt the
blood going through his veins.

12

ONE NIGHT, LATE July of summer fifteen, I went swimming
at the tiny beach. Alone.

Where were Gat, Johnny, and Mirren?

I don't really know.

We had been playing a lot of Scrabble at Red Gate. They
were probably there. Or they could have been at Clairmont,
listening to the aunts argue and eating beach plum jam on
water crackers.

In any case, I went into the water wearing a camisole,
bra, and underwear. Apparently I walked down to the beach

wearing nothing more. We never found any of my clothes on the sand. No towel, either.

Why?

Again, I don't really know.

I must have swum out far. There are big rocks in off the shore, craggy and black; they always look villainous in the dark of the evening. I must have had my face in the water and then hit my head on one of these rocks.

Like I said, I don't know.

I remember only this: I plunged down into this ocean,

down to rocky rocky bottom, and

I could see the base of Beechwood Island and

my arms and legs felt numb but my fingers were cold. Slices of seaweed went past as I fell.

Mummy found me on the sand, curled into a ball and half underwater. I was shivering uncontrollably. Adults wrapped me in blankets. They tried to get me warm at Cuddledown. They fed me tea and gave me clothes, but when I didn't talk or stop shivering, they brought me to a hospital on Martha's Vineyard, where I stayed for several days as the doctors ran tests. Hypothermia, respiratory problems, and most likely some kind of head injury, though the brain scans turned up nothing.

Mummy stayed by my side, got a hotel room. I remember the sad, gray faces of Aunt Carrie, Aunt Bess, and Granddad. I remember my lungs felt full of something, long after the doctors judged them clear. I remember I felt like I'd never get warm again, even when they told me my body temperature was normal. My hands hurt. My feet hurt.

Mummy took me home to Vermont to recuperate. I lay in bed in the dark and felt desperately sorry for myself. Because I was sick, and even more because Gat never called.

He didn't write, either.

Weren't we in love?

Weren't we?

I wrote to Johnny, two or three stupid, lovesick emails asking him to find out about Gat.

Johnny had the good sense to ignore them. We are Sinclairs, after all, and Sinclairs do not behave like I was behaving.

I stopped writing and deleted all the emails from my sent mail folder. They were weak and stupid.

The bottom line is, Gat bailed when I got hurt.

The bottom line is, it was only a summer fling.

The bottom line is, he might have loved Raquel.

We lived too far apart, anyway.

Our families were too close, anyway.

I never got an explanation.

I just know he left me.

13

WELCOME TO MY skull.

A truck is rolling over the bones of my neck and head. The vertebrae break, the brains pop and ooze. A thousand flashlights shine in my eyes. The world tilts.

I throw up. I black out.

This happens all the time. It's nothing but an ordinary day.

The pain started six weeks after my accident. Nobody was certain whether the two were related, but there was no denying the vomiting and weight loss and general horror.

Mummy took me for MRIs and CT scans. Needles, machines. More needles, more machines. They tested me for brain tumors, meningitis, you name it. To relieve the pain they prescribed this drug and that drug and another drug, because the first one didn't work and the second one didn't work, either. They gave me prescription after prescription without even knowing what was wrong. Just trying to quell the pain.

Cadence, said the doctors, don't take too much.

Cadence, said the doctors, watch for signs of addiction.

And still, Cadence, be sure to take your meds.

There were so many appointments I can't even remember them. Eventually the doctors came through with a diagnosis. Cadence Sinclair Eastman: post-traumatic headaches, also known as PTHA. Migraine headaches caused by traumatic brain injury.

I'll be fine, they tell me.

I won't die.

It'll just hurt a lot.

14

AFTER A YEAR in Colorado, Dad wanted to see me again. In fact, he insisted on taking me to Italy, France, Germany, Spain, and Scotland—a ten-week trip beginning in mid-June, which meant I wouldn't go to Beechwood at all, summer sixteen.

"The trip is grand timing," said Mummy brightly as she packed my suitcase.

"Why?" I lay on the floor of my bedroom and let her do the work. My head hurt.

"Granddad's redoing Clairmont." She rolled socks into balls. "I told you that a million times already."

I didn't remember. "How come?"

"Some idea of his. He's spending the summer in Windemere."

"With you waiting on him?"

Mummy nodded. "He can't stay with Bess or Carrie. And you know he takes looking after. Anyway. You'll get a wonderful education in Europe."

"I'd rather go to Beechwood."

"No, you wouldn't," she said, firm.

IN EUROPE, I vomited into small buckets and brushed my teeth repeatedly with chalky British toothpaste. I lay prone on the bathroom floors of several museums, feeling the cold tile underneath my cheek as my brain liquefied and seeped out my ear, bubbling. Migraines left my blood spreading across unfamiliar hotel sheets, dripping on the floors, oozing into carpets, soaking through leftover croissants and Italian lace cookies.

I could hear Dad calling me, but I never answered until my medicine took effect.

I missed the Liars that summer.

We never kept in touch over the school year. Not much, anyway, though we'd tried when we were younger. We'd text, or tag each other in summer photos, especially in September, but we'd inevitably fade out after a month or so. Somehow, Beechwood's magic never carried over into our everyday lives. We didn't want to hear about school friends and clubs and sports teams. Instead, we knew our affection would revive when we saw one another on the dock the following June, salt spray in the air, pale sun glinting off the water.

But the year after my accident, I missed days and even weeks of school. I failed my classes, and the principal informed me I would have to repeat junior year. I stopped soccer and tennis. I couldn't babysit. I couldn't drive. The friends I'd had weakened into acquaintances.

I texted Mirren a few times. Called and left her messages that later I was ashamed of, they were so lonely and needy.

I called Johnny, too, but his voice mail was full.

I decided not to call again. I didn't want to keep saying things that made me feel weak.

When Dad took me to Europe, I knew the Liars were on-island. Granddad hasn't wired Beechwood and cell phones don't get reception there, so I began writing emails. Different from my pitiful voice messages, these were charming, darling notes from a person without headaches.

Mostly.

Mirren!

Waving at you from Barcelona, where my father ate snails in broth.

Our hotel has gold everything. Even saltshakers. It is gloriously vile.

Write and tell me how the littles are misbehaving and where you are applying to college and whether you have found true love.

/Cadence

Johnny!

Bonjour from Paris, where my father ate a frog.
I saw the *Winged Victory*. Phenomenal body. No arms.
Miss you guys. How is Gat?

/Cadence

• • •

Mirren!

Hello from a castle in Scotland, where my father ate a haggis.
That is, my father ate the heart, liver, and lungs of a sheep mixed
with oatmeal and boiled in a sheep stomach.
So, you know, he is the sort of person who eats hearts.

/Cadence

• • •

Johnny!

I am in Berlin, where my father ate a blood sausage.
Snorkel for me. Eat blueberry pie. Play tennis. Build a bonfire.
Then report back. I am desperately bored and will devise
creative punishments if you do not comply.

/Cadence

I WASN'T ENTIRELY surprised they didn't answer. Besides
the fact that to get online you have to go to the Vineyard,
Beechwood is very much its own world. Once you are there,

the rest of the universe seems nothing but an unpleasant dream.

Europe might not even exist.

15

WELCOME, ONCE AGAIN, to the beautiful Sinclair family.

We believe in outdoor exercise. We believe that time heals.

We believe, although we will not say so explicitly, in prescription drugs and the cocktail hour.

We do not discuss our problems in restaurants. We do not believe in displays of distress. Our upper lips are stiff, and it is possible people are curious about us because we do not show them our hearts.

It is possible that we enjoy the way people are curious about us.

Here in Burlington, it's just me, Mummy, and the dogs now. We haven't the weight of Granddad in Boston or the impact of the whole family on Beechwood, but I know how people see us nonetheless. Mummy and I are two of a kind, in the big house with the porch at the top of the hill. The willowy mother and the sickly daughter. We are high of cheekbone, broad of shoulder. We smile and show our teeth when we run errands in town.

The sickly daughter doesn't talk much. People who know her at school tend to keep away. They didn't know her well before she got sick anyway. She was quiet even then.

Now she misses school half the time. When she's there, her pale skin and watery eyes make her look glamorously tragic, like a literary heroine wasting from consumption. Sometimes she falls down at school, crying. She frightens the other students. Even the kindest ones are tired of walking her to the nurse's office.

Still, she has an aura of mystery that stops her from being teased or singled out for typical high school unpleasantness. Her mother is a Sinclair.

Of course, I feel no sense of my own mystery eating a can of chicken soup late at night, or lying in the fluorescent light of the school nurse's office. It is hardly glamorous the way Mummy and I quarrel now that Dad is gone.

I wake to find her standing in my bedroom doorway, staring. "Don't hover."

"I love you. I'm taking care of you," she says, her hand on her heart.

"Well, stop it."

If I could shut my door on her, I would. But I cannot stand up.

Often I find notes lying around that appear to be records of what foods I've eaten on a particular day: *Toast and jam, but only 1/2; apple and popcorn; salad with raisins; chocolate bar; pasta. Hydration? Protein? Too much ginger ale.*

It is not glamorous that I can't drive a car. It is not mysterious to be home on a Saturday night, reading a novel in a pile of smelly golden retrievers. However, I am not immune to the feeling of being *viewed* as a mystery, as a Sinclair, as part of a privileged clan of special people, and as part of a magical, important narrative, just because I am part of this clan.

My mother is not immune to it, either.

This is who we have been brought up to be.

Sinclairs. Sinclairs.

PART TWO
Vermont

16

WHEN I WAS eight, Dad gave me a stack of fairy-tale books for Christmas. They came with colored covers: *The Yellow Fairy Book, The Blue Fairy Book, The Crimson, The Green, The Gray, The Brown,* and *The Orange.* Inside were tales from all over the world, variations on variations of familiar stories.

Read them and you hear echoes of one story inside another, then echoes of another inside that. So many have the same premise: once upon a time, there were three.

Three of something:

three pigs,

three bears,

three brothers,

three soldiers,

three billy goats.

Three princesses.

Since I got back from Europe, I have been writing some of my own. Variations.

I have time on my hands, so let me tell you a story. A variation, I am saying, of a story you have heard before.

ONCE UPON *A time there was a king who had three beautiful daughters.*

As he grew old, he began to wonder which should inherit the kingdom, since none had married and he had no heir. The

43

king decided to ask his daughters to demonstrate their love for him.

To the eldest princess he said, "Tell me how you love me."

She loved him as much as all the treasure in the kingdom.

To the middle princess he said, "Tell me how you love me."

She loved him with the strength of iron.

To the youngest princess he said, "Tell me how you love me."

This youngest princess thought for a long time before answering. Finally she said she loved him as meat loves salt.

"Then you do not love me at all," the king said. He threw his daughter from the castle and had the bridge drawn up behind her so that she could not return.

Now, this youngest princess goes into the forest with not so much as a coat or a loaf of bread. She wanders through a hard winter, taking shelter beneath trees. She arrives at an inn and gets hired as assistant to the cook. As the days and weeks go by, the princess learns the ways of the kitchen. Eventually she surpasses her employer in skill and her food is known throughout the land.

Years pass, and the eldest princess comes to be married. For the festivities, the cook from the inn makes the wedding meal.

Finally a large roast pig is served. It is the king's favorite dish, but this time it has been cooked with no salt.

The king tastes it.

Tastes it again.

"Who would dare to serve such an ill-cooked roast at the future queen's wedding?" he cries.

The princess-cook appears before her father, but she is so changed he does not recognize her. "I would not serve you salt, Your Majesty," she explains. "For did you not exile your youngest daughter for saying that it was of value?"

At her words, the king realizes that not only is she his daughter—she is, in fact, the daughter who loves him best.

And what then?

The eldest daughter and the middle sister have been living with the king all this time. One has been in favor one week, the other the next. They have been driven apart by their father's constant comparisons. Now the youngest has returned, the king yanks the kingdom from his eldest, who has just been married. She is not to be queen after all. The elder sisters rage.

At first, the youngest basks in fatherly love. Before long, however, she realizes the king is demented and power-mad. She is to be queen, but she is also stuck tending to a crazy old tyrant for the rest of her days. She will not leave him, no matter how sick he becomes.

Does she stay because she loves him as meat loves salt?

Or does she stay because he has now promised her the kingdom?

It is hard for her to tell the difference.

17

THE FALL AFTER the European trip, I started a project. I give away something of mine every day.

I mailed Mirren an old Barbie with extra-long hair, one we used to fight over when we were kids. I mailed Johnny a striped scarf I used to wear a lot. Johnny likes stripes.

For the old people in my family—Mummy, the aunties,

Granddad—the accumulation of beautiful objects is a life goal. Whoever dies with the most stuff wins.

Wins *what*? is what I'd like to know.

I used to be a person who liked pretty things. Like Mummy does, like all the Sinclairs do. But that's not me anymore.

Mummy has our Burlington house filled with silver and crystal, coffee-table books and cashmere blankets. Thick rugs cover every floor, and paintings from several local artists she patronizes line our walls. She likes antique china and displays it in the dining room. She's replaced the perfectly drivable Saab with a BMW.

Not one of these symbols of prosperity and taste has any use at all.

"Beauty is a valid use," Mummy argues. "It creates a sense of place, a sense of personal history. Pleasure, even, Cadence. Have you ever heard of pleasure?"

But I think she's lying, to me and to herself, about why she owns these objects. The jolt of a new purchase makes Mummy feel powerful, if only for a moment. I think there is status to having a house full of pretty things, to buying expensive paintings of seashells from her arty friends and spoons from Tiffany's. Antiques and Oriental rugs tell people that my mother may be a dog breeder who dropped out of Bryn Mawr, but she's got power—because she's got money.

GIVEAWAY: MY BED pillow. I carry it while I run errands.

There is a girl leaning against the wall outside the library. She has a cardboard cup by her ankles for spare change. She is not much older than I am.

"Do you want this pillow?" I ask. "I washed the pillowcase."

She takes it and sits on it.

My bed is uncomfortable that night, but it's for the best.

GIVEAWAY: PAPERBACK COPY of King Lear I read for school sophomore year, found under the bed.

Donated to the public library.

I don't need to read it again.

GIVEAWAY: A PHOTO of Granny Tipper at the Farm Institute party, wearing an evening dress and holding a piglet.

I stop by Goodwill on my way home. "Hey there, Cadence," says Patti behind the counter. "Just dropping off?"

"This was my Gran."

"She was a beautiful lady," says Patti, peering. "You sure you don't want to take the photo out? You could donate just the frame."

"I'm sure."

Gran is dead. Having a picture of her won't change anything.

"DID YOU GO by Goodwill again?" Mummy asks when I get home. She is slicing peaches with a special fruit knife.

"Yeah."

"What did you get rid of?"

"Just an old picture of Gran."

"With the piglet?" Her mouth twitches. "Oh, Cady."

"It was mine to give away."

Mummy sighs. "You give away one of the dogs and you will never hear the end of it."

I squat down to dog height. Bosh, Grendel, and Poppy greet me with soft, indoor woofs. They're our family dogs, portly and well-behaved. Purebred goldens. Poppy had several litters for my mother's business, but the puppies and the other breeding dogs live with Mummy's partner at a farm outside Burlington.

"I would never," I say.

I whisper how I love them into their soft doggy ears.

18

IF I GOOGLE *traumatic brain injury*, most websites tell me selective amnesia is a consequence. When there's damage to the brain, it's not uncommon for a patient to forget stuff. She will be unable to piece together a coherent story of the trauma.

But I don't want people to know I'm like this. Still like this, after all the appointments and scans and medicines.

I don't want to be labeled with a disability. I don't want more drugs. I don't want doctors or concerned teachers. God knows, I've had enough doctors.

What I remember, from the summer of the accident:

Falling in love with Gat at the Red Gate kitchen door.

His beach rose for Raquel and my wine-soaked night, spinning in anger.

Acting normal. Making ice cream. Playing tennis.

The triple-decker s'mores and Gat's anger when we told him to shut up.

Night swimming.

Kissing Gat in the attic.

Hearing the Cracker Jack story and helping Granddad down the stairs.

The tire swing, the basement, the perimeter. Gat and I in one another's arms.

Gat seeing me bleed. Asking me questions. Dressing my wounds.

I don't remember much else.

I can see Mirren's hand, her chipped gold nail polish, holding a jug of gas for the motorboats.

Mummy, her face tight, asking, "The black pearls?"

Johnny's feet, running down the stairs from Clairmont to the boathouse.

Granddad, holding on to a tree, his face lit by the glow of a bonfire.

And all four of us Liars, laughing so hard we felt dizzy and sick. But what was so funny?

What was it and where were we?

I do not know.

I used to ask Mummy when I didn't remember the rest of summer fifteen. My forgetfulness frightened me. I'd suggest stopping my meds, or trying new meds, or seeing a different physician. I'd beg to know what I'd forgotten. Then one day in late fall—the fall I spent undergoing tests for death-sentence illnesses—Mummy began to cry. "You ask me over and over. You never remember what I say."

"I'm sorry."

She poured herself a glass of wine as she talked. "You began asking me the day you woke in the hospital. 'What happened? What happened?' I told you the truth, Cadence, I always did, and you'd repeat it back to me. But the next day you'd ask again."

"I'm sorry," I said again.

"You still ask me almost every day."

It is true, I have no memory of my accident. I don't remember what happened before and after. I don't remember my doctor's visits. I knew they must have happened, because of course they happened—and here I am with a diagnosis and medications—but nearly all my medical treatment is a blank.

I looked at Mummy. At her infuriatingly concerned face, her leaking eyes, the tipsy slackness of her mouth. "You have to stop asking," she said. "The doctors think it's better if you remember on your own, anyway."

I made her tell me one last time, and I wrote down her answers so I could look back at them when I wanted to. That's why I can tell you about the night-swimming accident, the rocks, the hypothermia, respiratory difficulty, and the unconfirmed traumatic brain injury.

I never asked her anything again. There's a lot I don't understand, but this way she stays pretty sober.

19

DAD PLANS TO take me to Australia and New Zealand for the whole of summer seventeen.

I don't want to go.

I want to return to Beechwood. I want to see Mirren and lie

in the sun, planning our futures. I want to argue with Johnny and go snorkeling and make ice cream. I want to build bonfires on the shore of the tiny beach. I want to pile in the hammock on the Clairmont porch and be the Liars once again, if it's possible.

I want to remember my accident.

I want to know why Gat disappeared. I don't know why he wasn't with me, swimming. I don't know why I went to the tiny beach alone. Why I swam in my underwear and left no clothes on the sand. And why he bailed when I got hurt.

I wonder if he loved me. I wonder if he loved Raquel.

Dad and I are supposed to leave for Australia in five days.

I should never have agreed to go.

I make myself wretched, sobbing. I tell Mummy I don't need to see the world. I need to see family. I miss Granddad.

No.

I'll be sick if I travel to Australia. My headaches will explode, I shouldn't get on a plane. I shouldn't eat strange food. I shouldn't be jet-lagged. What if we lose my medication?

Stop arguing. The trip is paid for.

I walk the dogs in the early morning. I load the dishwasher and later unload it. I put on a dress and rub blusher into my cheeks. I eat everything on my plate. I let Mummy put her arms around me and stroke my hair. I tell her I want to spend the summer with her, not Dad.

Please.

The next day, Granddad comes to Burlington to stay in the guest room. He's been on the island since mid-May and has to take a boat, a car, and a plane to get here. He hasn't come to visit us since before Granny Tipper died.

Mummy picks him up at the airport while I stay home and set the table for supper. She's picked up roast chicken and side dishes at a gourmet shop in town.

Granddad has lost weight since I saw him last. His white hair stands out in puffs around his ears, tufty; he looks like a baby bird. His skin is baggy on his frame, and he has a potbellied slump that's not how I remember him. He always seemed invincible, with firm, broad shoulders and lots of teeth.

Granddad is the sort of person who has mottos. "Don't take no for an answer," he always says to us. And "Never take a seat in the back of the room. Winners sit up front."

We Liars used to roll our eyes at these pronouncements— "Be decisive; no one likes a waffler"; "Never complain, never explain"—but we still saw him as full of wisdom on grown-up topics.

Granddad is wearing madras shorts and loafers. His legs are spindly old-man legs. He pats my back and demands a scotch and soda.

We eat and he talks about some friends of his in Boston. The new kitchen in his Beechwood house. Nothing important. Afterward, Mummy cleans up while I show him the backyard garden. The evening sun is still out.

Granddad picks a peony and hands it to me. "For my first grandchild."

"Don't pick the flowers, okay?"

"Penny won't mind."

"Yes, she will."

"Cadence was the first," he says, looking up at the sky, not into my eyes. "I remember when she came to visit us in Boston. She was dressed in a pink romper suit and her hair stuck

52

up straight off her head. Johnny wasn't born till three weeks later."

"I'm right here, Granddad."

"Cadence was the first, and it didn't matter that she was a girl. I would give her everything. Just like a grandson. I carried her in my arms and danced. She was the future of our family."

I nod.

"We could see she was a Sinclair. She had that hair, but it wasn't only that. It was the chin, the tiny hands. We knew she'd be tall. All of us were tall until Bess married that short fellow, and Carrie made the same mistake."

"You mean Brody and William."

"Good riddance, eh?" Granddad smiles. "All our people were tall. Did you know my mother's side of the family came over on the *Mayflower*? To make this life in America."

I know it's not important if our people came over on the *Mayflower*. It's not important to be tall. Or blond. That is why I dyed my hair: I don't want to be the eldest. Heiress to the island, the fortune, and the expectations.

But then again, perhaps I do.

Granddad has had too much to drink after a long travel day. "Shall we go inside?" I ask. "You want to sit down?"

He picks a second peony and hands it to me. "For forgiveness, my dear."

I pat him on his hunched back. "Don't pick any more, okay?"

Granddad bends down and touches some white tulips.

"Seriously, don't," I say.

He picks a third peony, sharply, defiantly. Hands it to me. "You are my Cadence. The first."

"Yes."

"What happened to your hair?"

"I colored it."

"I didn't recognize you."

"That's okay."

Granddad points to the peonies, now all in my hand. "Three flowers for you. You should have three."

He looks pitiful. He looks powerful.

I love him, but I am not sure I like him. I take his hand and lead him inside.

20

ONCE UPON A time, there was a king who had three beautiful daughters. He loved each of them dearly. One day, when the young ladies were of age to be married, a terrible, three-headed dragon laid siege to the kingdom, burning villages with fiery breath. It spoiled crops and burned churches. It killed babies, old people, and everyone in between.

The king promised a princess's hand in marriage to whoever slayed the dragon. Heroes and warriors came in suits of armor, riding brave horses and bearing swords and arrows.

One by one, these men were slaughtered and eaten.

Finally the king reasoned that a maiden might melt the dragon's heart and succeed where warriors had failed. He sent his eldest daughter to beg the dragon for mercy, but the dragon listened to not a word of her pleas. It swallowed her whole.

Then the king sent his second daughter to beg the dragon for *mercy, but the dragon did the same. Swallowed her before she could get a word out.*

The king then sent his youngest daughter to beg the dragon for mercy, and she was so lovely and clever that he was sure she would succeed where the others had perished.

No indeed. The dragon simply ate her.

The king was left aching with regret. He was now alone in the world.

Now, let me ask you this. Who killed the girls?

The dragon? Or their father?

AFTER GRANDDAD LEAVES the next day, Mummy calls Dad and cancels the Australia trip. There is yelling. There is negotiation.

Eventually they decide I will go to Beechwood for four weeks of the summer, then visit Dad at his home in Colorado, where I've never been. He insists. He will not lose the whole summer with me or there will be lawyers involved.

Mummy rings the aunts. She has long, private conversations with them on the porch of our house. I can't hear anything except a few phrases: Cadence is so fragile, needs lots of rest. Only four weeks, not the whole summer. Nothing should disturb her, the healing is very gradual.

Also, pinot grigio, Sancerre, maybe some Riesling; definitely no chardonnay.

21

MY ROOM IS nearly empty now. There are sheets and a comforter on my bed. A laptop on my desk, a few pens. A chair.

I own a couple pairs of jeans and shorts. I have T-shirts and flannel shirts, some warm sweaters; a bathing suit, a pair of sneakers, a pair of Crocs, and a pair of boots. Two dresses and some heels. Warm coat, hunting jacket, and canvas duffel.

The shelves are bare. No pictures, no posters. No old toys.

GIVEAWAY: A TRAVEL toothbrush kit Mummy bought me yesterday.

I already have a toothbrush. I don't know why she would buy me another. That woman buys things just to buy things. It's disgusting.

I walk over to the library and find the girl who took my pillow. She's still leaning against the outside wall. I set the toothbrush kit in her cup.

GIVEAWAY: GAT'S OLIVE hunting jacket. The one I wore that night we held hands and looked at the stars and talked about God. I never returned it.

I should have given it away first of everything. I know that. But I couldn't make myself. It was all I had left of him.

But that was weak and foolish. Gat doesn't love me.

I don't love him, either, and maybe I never did.

I'll see him day after tomorrow and I don't love him and I don't want his jacket.

22

THE PHONE RINGS at ten the night before we leave for Beechwood. Mummy is in the shower. I pick up.

Heavy breathing. Then a laugh.

"Who is this?"

"Cady?"

It's a kid, I realize. "Yes."

"This is Taft." Mirren's brother. He has no manners.

"How come you're awake?"

"Is it true you're a drug addict?" Taft asks me.

"No."

"Are you sure?"

"You're calling to ask if I'm a drug addict?" I haven't talked to Taft since my accident.

"We're on Beechwood," he says. "We got here this morning."

I am glad he's changing the subject. I make my voice bright. "We're coming tomorrow. Is it nice? Did you go swimming yet?"

"No."

"Did you go on the tire swing?"

"No," says Taft. "Are you sure you're not a drug addict?"

"Where did you even get that idea?"

"Bonnie. She says I should watch out for you."

"Don't listen to Bonnie," I say. "Listen to Mirren."

"That's what I'm talking about. But Bonnie's the only one who believes me about Cuddledown," he says. "And I wanted to call you. Only not if you're a drug addict because drug addicts don't know what's going on."

"I'm not a drug addict, you pipsqueak," I say. Though possibly I am lying.

"Cuddledown is haunted," says Taft. "Can I come and sleep with you at Windemere?"

I like Taft. I do. He's slightly bonkers and covered with freckles and Mirren loves him way more than she loves the twins. "It's not haunted. The wind just blows through the house," I say. "It blows through Windemere, too. The windows rattle."

"It is too, haunted," Taft says. "Mummy doesn't believe me and neither does Liberty."

When he was younger he was always the kid who thought there were monsters in the closet. Later he was convinced there was a sea monster under the dock.

"Ask Mirren to help you," I tell him. "She'll read you a bedtime story or sing to you."

"You think so?"

"She will. And when I get there I'll take you tubing and snorkeling and it'll be a grand summer, Taft."

"Okay," he says.

"Don't be scared of stupid old Cuddledown," I tell him. "Show it who's boss and I'll see you tomorrow."

He hangs up without saying goodbye.

PART THREE
Summer Seventeen

23

IN WOODS HOLE, the port town, Mummy and I let the goldens out of the car and drag our bags down to where Aunt Carrie is standing on the dock.

Carrie gives Mummy a long hug before she helps us load our bags and the dogs into the big motorboat. "You're more beautiful than ever," she says. "And thank God you're here."

"Oh, quiet," says Mummy.

"I know you've been sick," Carrie says to me. She is the tallest of my aunts, and the eldest Sinclair daughter. Her sweater is long and cashmere. The lines on the sides of her mouth are deep. She's wearing some ancient jade jewelry that belonged to Gran.

"Nothing wrong with me that a Percocet and a couple slugs of vodka doesn't cure," I say.

Carrie laughs, but Mummy leans in and says, "She's not taking Percocet. She's taking a nonaddictive medicine the doctor prescribes."

It isn't true. The nonaddictive medicines didn't work.

"She looks too thin," says Carrie.

"It's all the vodka," I say. "It fills me up."

"She can't eat much when she's hurting," says Mummy. "The pain makes her nauseated."

"Bess made that blueberry pie you like," Aunt Carrie tells me. She gives Mummy another hug.

"You guys are so huggy all of a sudden," I say. "You never used to be huggy."

Aunt Carrie hugs me, too. She smells of expensive, lemony perfume. I haven't seen her in a long time.

The drive out of the harbor is cold and sparkly. I sit at the back of the boat while Mummy stands next to Aunt Carrie behind the wheel. I trail my hand in the water. It sprays the arm of my duffel coat, soaking the canvas.

I will see Gat soon.

Gat, my Gat, who is not my Gat.

The houses. The littles, the aunts, the Liars.

I will hear the sound of seagulls, taste slumps and pie and homemade ice cream. I'll hear the pong of tennis balls, the bark of goldens, the echo of my breath in a snorkel. We'll make bonfires that will smell of ashes.

Will I still be at home?

Before long, Beechwood is ahead of us, the familiar outline looming. The first house I see is Windemere with its multitude of peaked roofs. That room on the far right is Mummy's; there are her pale blue curtains. My own window looks to the inside of the island.

Carrie steers the boat around the tip and I can see Cuddledown there at the lowest point of the land, with its chubby, boxlike structure. A bitty, sandy cove—the tiny beach—is tucked in at the bottom of a long wooden staircase.

The view changes as we circle to the eastern side of the island. I can't see much of Red Gate among the trees, but I glimpse its red trim. Then the big beach, accessed by another wooden staircase.

Clairmont sits at the highest point, with water views in three directions. I crane my neck to look for its friendly turret—

but it isn't there. The trees that used to shade the big, sloping yard—they're gone, too. Instead of the Victorian six-bedroom with the wraparound porch and the farmhouse kitchen, instead of the house where Granddad spent every summer since forever, I see a sleek modern building perched on a rocky hill. There's a Japanese garden on one side, bare rock on the other. The house is glass and iron. Cold.

Carrie cuts the engine down, which makes it easier to talk. "That's New Clairmont," she says.

"It was just a shell last year. I never imagined he wouldn't have a lawn," says Mummy.

"Wait till you see the inside. The walls are bare, and when we got here yesterday, he had nothing in the fridge but some apples and a wedge of Havarti."

"Since when does he even like Havarti?" asks Mummy. "Havarti isn't even a good cheese."

"He doesn't know how to shop. Ginny and Lucille, that's the new cook, only do what he tells them to do. He's been eating cheese toast. But I made a huge list and they went to the Edgartown market. We have enough for a few days now."

Mummy shivers. "It's good we're here."

I stare at the new building while the aunts talk. I knew Granddad renovated, of course. He and Mummy talked about the new kitchen when he visited just a few days ago. The fridge and the extra freezer, the warming drawer and spice racks.

I didn't realize he'd torn the house down. That the lawn was gone. And the trees, especially the huge old maple with the tire swing beneath it. That tree must have been a hundred years old.

A wave surges up, dark blue, leaping from the sea like a whale. It arches over me. The muscles of my neck spasm, my throat catches. I fold beneath the weight of it. The blood rushes to my head. I am drowning.

It all seems so sad, so unbearably sad for a second, to think of the lovely old maple with the swing. We never told the tree how much we loved it. We never gave it a name, never did anything for it. It could have lived so much longer.

I am so, so cold.

"Cadence?" Mummy is leaning over me.

I reach and clutch her hand.

"Be normal now," she whispers. "Right now."

"What?"

"Because you are. Because you can be."

Okay. Okay. It was just a tree.

Just a tree with a tire swing that I loved a lot.

"Don't cause a scene," whispers Mummy. "Breathe and sit up."

I do what she asks as soon as I am able, just as I have always done.

Aunt Carrie provides distraction, speaking brightly. "The new garden is nice, when you get used to it," she says. "There's a seating area for cocktail hour. Taft and Will are finding special rocks."

She turns the boat toward the shore and suddenly I can see my Liars waiting, not on the dock but by the weathered wooden fence that runs along the perimeter path.

Mirren stands with her feet on the lower half of the barrier, waving joyfully, her hair whipping in the wind.

Mirren. She is sugar. She is curiosity and rain.

Johnny jumps up and down, every now and then doing a cartwheel.

Johnny. He is bounce. He is effort and snark.

Gat, my Gat, once upon a time my Gat—he has come out to see me, too. He stands back from the slats of the fence, on the rocky hill that now leads to Clairmont. He's doing pretend semaphore, waving his arms in ornate patterns as if I'm supposed to understand some kind of secret code. He is contemplation and enthusiasm. Ambition and strong coffee.

Welcome home, they are saying. Welcome home.

24

THE LIARS DON'T come to the dock when we pull in, and neither do Aunt Bess and Granddad. Instead, it is only the littles: Will and Taft, Liberty and Bonnie.

The boys, both ten, kick one another and wrestle around. Taft runs over and grabs my arm. I pick him up and spin him. He is surprisingly light, like his freckled body is made of bird parts. "You feeling better?" I ask.

"We have ice cream bars in the freezer!" he yells. "Three different kinds!"

"Seriously, Taft. You were a mess on the phone last night."

"Was not."

"Were too."

"Mirren read me a story. Then I went to sleep. No big whup."

I ruffle his honey hair. "It's just a house. Lots of houses seem scary at night, but in the morning, they're friendly again."

"We're not staying at Cuddledown anyway," Taft says. "We moved to New Clairmont with Granddad now."

"You did?"

"We have to be orderly there and not act like idiots. We took our stuff already. And Will caught three jellyfish at the big beach and also a dead crab. Will you come see them?"

"Sure."

"He has the crab in his pocket, but the jellies are in a bucket of water," says Taft, and runs off.

MUMMY AND I walk across the island to Windemere, a short distance on a wooden walkway. The twins help with our suitcases.

Granddad and Aunt Bess are in the kitchen. There are wildflowers in vases on the counter, and Bess scrubs a clean sink with a Brillo pad while Granddad reads the *Martha's Vineyard Times*.

Bess is softer than her sisters, and blonder, but still the same mold. She's wearing white jeans and a navy blue cotton top with diamond jewelry. She takes off rubber gloves and then kisses Mummy and hugs me too long and too hard, like she is trying to hug some deep and secret message. She smells of bleach and wine.

Granddad stands up but doesn't cross the room until Bess is done hugging. "Hello there, Mirren," he says jovially. "Grand to see you."

"He's doing that a lot," Carrie says to me and Mummy. "Calling people Mirren who aren't Mirren."

"I know she's not Mirren," Granddad says.

The adults talk amongst themselves, and I am left with the twins. They look awkward in Crocs and summer dresses. They must be almost fourteen now. They have Mirren's strong legs and blue eyes but their faces are pinched.

"Your hair is black," says Bonnie. "You look like a dead vampire."

"Bonnie!" Liberty smacks her.

"I mean, that's redundant because *all* vampires are dead," says Bonnie. "But they have the circles under their eyes and the white skin, like you do."

"Be nice to Cady," whispers Liberty. "Mom told us."

"I am being nice," says Bonnie. "A lot of vampires are extremely sexy. That's a documented fact."

"I told you I didn't want you talking about creepy dead stuff this summer," says Liberty. "You were bad enough last night." She turns to me. "Bonnie's obsessed with dead things. She's reading books about them all the time and then she can't sleep. It's annoying when you share a room." Liberty says all this without ever looking me in the eye.

"I was talking about Cady's hair," says Bonnie.

"You don't have to tell her she looks dead."

"It's okay," I tell Bonnie. "I don't actually care what you think, so it's perfectly okay."

25

EVERYONE HEADS TO New Clairmont, leaving me and Mummy alone at Windemere to unpack. I ditch my bag and look for the Liars.

Suddenly they are on me like puppies. Mirren grabs me and spins me. Johnny grabs Mirren, Gat grabs Johnny, we are all grabbing each other and jumping. Then we are apart again, going into Cuddledown.

Mirren chatters about how glad she is that Bess and the littles will live with Granddad this summer. He needs somebody with him now. Plus Bess with her obsessive cleaning is impossible to be around. Plus again and even more important, we Liars will have Cuddledown to ourselves. Gat says he is going to make hot tea and hot tea is his new vice. Johnny calls him a pretentious assface. We follow Gat into the kitchen. He puts water on to boil.

It is a whirlwind, all of them talking over each other, arguing happily, exactly like old times. Gat hasn't quite looked at me, though.

I can't stop looking at him.

He is so beautiful. So Gat. I know the arc of his lower lip, the strength in his shoulders. The way he half tucks his shirt into his jeans, the way his shoes are worn down at the heel, the way he touches that scar on his eyebrow without realizing he's doing it.

I am so angry. And so happy to see him.

Probably he has moved on, like any well-adjusted person would. Gat hasn't spent the last two years in a shell of headache pain and self-pity. He's been going around with New York City girls in ballet flats, taking them to Chinese food and out to see bands. If he's not with Raquel, he's probably got a girl or even three at home.

"Your hair's new," Johnny says to me.

"Yeah."

"You look pretty, though," says Mirren sweetly.

"She's so tall," says Gat, busying himself with boxes of tea, jasmine and English Breakfast and so on. "You didn't used to be that tall, did you, Cady?"

"It's called growing," I say. "Don't hold me responsible."
Two summers ago, Gat was several inches taller than I. Now
we are about even.

"I'm all for growing," says Gat, his eyes still not on my face.
"Just don't get taller than me."

Is he flirting?

He is.

"Johnny always lets me be tallest," Gat goes on. "Never
makes an issue of it."

"Like I have a choice," groans Johnny.

"She's still our Cady," says Mirren loyally. "We probably
look different to her, too."

But they don't. They look the same. Gat in a worn green
T-shirt from two summers ago. His ready smile, his way of
leaning forward, his dramatic nose.

Johnny broad-shouldered, in jeans and a pink plaid button-
down so old its edges are frayed; nails bitten, hair cropped.

Mirren, like a pre-Raphaelite painting, that square Sinclair
chin. Her long, thick hair is piled on top of her head and she's
wearing a bikini top and shorts.

It is reassuring. I love them so.

Will it matter to them, the way I can't hold on to even basic
facts surrounding my accident? I've lost so much of what we
did together summer fifteen. I wonder if the aunts have been
talking about me.

I don't want them to look at me like I'm sick. Or like my
mind isn't working.

"Tell about college," says Johnny. He is sitting on the kitchen
counter. "Where are you going?"

"Nowhere, yet." This truth I can't avoid. I am surprised they
don't know it already.

"What?"

"Why?"

"I didn't graduate. I missed too much school after the accident."

"Oh, barf!" yells Johnny. "That is horrible. You can't do summer school?"

"Not and come here. Besides, I'll do better if I apply with all my coursework done."

"What are you going to study?" asks Gat.

"Let's talk about something else."

"But we want to know," says Mirren. "We all do."

"Seriously," I say. "Something else. How's your love life, Johnny?"

"Barf again."

I raise my eyebrows.

"When you're as handsome as I am, the course never runs smooth," he quips.

"I have a boyfriend named Drake Loggerhead," says Mirren. "He's going to Pomona like I am. We have had sexual intercourse quite a number of times, but always with protection. He brings me yellow roses every week and has nice muscles."

Johnny spits out his tea. Gat and I laugh.

"Drake Loggerhead?" Johnny asks.

"Yes," says Mirren. "What's so funny?"

"Nothing." Johnny shakes his head.

"We've been going out five months," says Mirren. "He's spending the summer doing Outward Bound, so he'll have even more muscles when I see him next!"

"You've got to be kidding," Gat says.

"Just a little," says Mirren. "But I love him."

I squeeze her hand. I am happy she has someone to be in

love with. "I'm going to ask you about the sexual intercourse later," I warn her.

"When the boys aren't here," she says. "I'll tell you all."

We leave our teacups and walk down to the tiny beach. Take our shoes off and wiggle our toes in the sand. There are tiny, sharp shells.

"I'm not going to supper at New Clairmont," says Mirren decisively. "And no breakfast, either. Not this year."

"Why not?" I ask.

"I can't take it," she says. "The aunts. The littles. Granddad. He's lost his mind, you know."

I nod.

"It's too much togetherness. I just want to be happy with you guys, down here," says Mirren. "I'm not hanging around in that cold new house. Those people are fine without me."

"Same," says Johnny.

"Same," says Gat.

I realize they discussed this idea before I arrived.

26

MIRREN AND JOHNNY go in the water with snorkels and fins. They kick around looking for lobsters. Probably there are only jellyfish and tiny crabs, but even with those slim pickings we have snorkeled at the tiny beach, always.

Gat sits with me on a batik blanket. We watch the others in silence.

I don't know how to talk to him.

I love him.

He's been an ass.

I shouldn't love him. I'm stupid for still loving him. I have to forget about it.

Maybe he still thinks I am pretty. Even with my hair and the hollows beneath my eyes. Maybe.

The muscles of his back shift beneath his T-shirt. The curve of his neck, the soft arch of his ear. A little brown mole on the side of his neck. The moons of his fingernails. I drink him up after so long apart.

"Don't look at my troll feet," says Gat suddenly.

"What?"

"They're hideous. A troll snuck into my room at night, took my normal feet for himself, and left me with his thuggish troll feet." Gat tucks his feet under a towel so I can't see them. "Now you know the truth."

I am relieved we are talking about nothing important. "Wear shoes."

"I'm not wearing shoes on the beach." He wiggles his feet out from beneath the towel. They look fine. "I have to act like everything's okay until I can find that troll. Then I'll kill him to death and get my normal feet back. Have you got weapons?"

"No."

"Come on."

"Um. There's a fire poker in Windemere."

"All right. As soon as we see that troll, we'll kill him to death with your fire poker."

"If you insist."

I lie back on the blanket and put my arm over my eyes. We are silent for a moment.

"Trolls are nocturnal," I add.

"Cady?" Gat whispers.

I turn my face to look in his eyes. "Yeah?"

"I thought I might never see you again."

"What?" He is so close we could kiss.

"I thought I might never see you again. After everything that happened, then when you weren't here last summer."

Why didn't you write me? I want to say. Why didn't you call, all this time?

He touches my face. "I'm so glad you're here," he says. "I'm so glad I got the chance."

I don't know what is between us. I really don't. He is such an ass.

"Give me your hand," Gat says.

I am not sure I want to.

But then of course I do want to.

His skin is warm and sandy. We intertwine our fingers and close our eyes against the sun.

We just lie there. Holding hands. He rubs my palm with his thumb like he did two summers ago beneath the stars.

And I melt.

27

MY ROOM AT Windemere is wood-paneled, with cream paint. There's a green patchwork quilt on the bed. The carpet is one of those rag rugs you see in country inns.

You were here two summers ago, I tell myself. In this room, every night. In this room, every morning.

Presumably you were reading, playing games on the iPad, choosing clothes. What do you remember?

Nothing.

Tasteful botanic prints line the walls of my room, plus some art I made: a watercolor of the maple that used to loom over the Clairmont lawn, and two crayon drawings: one of Granny Tipper and her dogs, Prince Philip and Fatima; the other of my father. I drag the wicker laundry basket from the closet, take down all the pictures, and load them into the basket.

There's a bookshelf lined with paperbacks, teen books and fantasy I was into reading a few years back. Kids' stories I read a hundred times. I pull them down and stack them in the hallway.

"You're giving away the books? You love books," Mummy says. She's coming out of her room wearing fresh clothes for supper. Lipstick.

"We can give them to one of the Vineyard libraries," I say. "Or to Goodwill."

Mummy bends over and flips through the paperbacks. "We read *Charmed Life* together, do you remember?"

I nod.

"And this one, too. *The Lives of Christopher Chant*. That was the year you were eight. You wanted to read everything but you weren't a good enough reader yet, so I read to you and Gat for hours and hours."

"What about Johnny and Mirren?"

"They couldn't sit still," says Mummy. "Don't you want to keep these?"

She reaches out and touches my cheek. I pull back. "I want the things to find a better home," I tell her.

"I was hoping you would feel different when we came back to the island, is all."

"You got rid of all Dad's stuff. You bought a new couch, new dishes, new jewelry."

"Cady."

"There's nothing in our whole house that says he ever lived with us, except me. Why are you allowed to erase my father and I'm not allowed to—"

"Erase yourself?" Mummy says.

"Other people might use these," I snap, pointing at the stacks of books. "People who have actual needs. Don't you think of doing good in the world?"

At that moment, Poppy, Bosh, and Grendel hurtle upstairs and clog the hallway where we are standing, snarfling our hands, flapping their hairy tails at our knees.

Mummy and I are silent.

Finally she says, "It's all right for you to moon around at the tiny beach, or whatever you did this afternoon. It's all right for you to give away your books if you feel that strongly. But I expect you at Clairmont for supper in an hour with a smile on your face for Granddad. No arguments. No excuses. You understand me?"

I nod.

28

A PAD IS left from several summers ago when Gat and I got obsessed with graph paper. We made drawing after drawing on it by filling in the tiny squares with colored pencil to make pixelated portraits.

I find a pen and write down all my memories of summer fifteen.

The s'mores, the swim. The attic, the interruption.

Mirren's hand, her chipped gold nail polish, holding a jug of gas for the motorboats.

Mummy, her face tight, asking, "The black pearls?"

Johnny's feet, running down the stairs from Clairmont to the boathouse.

Granddad, holding on to a tree, his face lit by the glow of a bonfire.

And all four of us Liars, laughing so hard we felt dizzy and sick.

I make a separate page for the accident itself. What Mummy's told me and what I guess. I must have gone swimming on the tiny beach alone. I hit my head on a rock. I must have struggled back to shore. Aunt Bess and Mummy gave me tea. I was diagnosed with hypothermia, respiratory problems, and a brain injury that never showed on the scans.

I tack the pages to the wall above my bed. I add sticky notes with questions.

Why did I go into the water alone at night?

Where were my clothes?

Did I really have a head injury from the swim, or did something else happen? Could someone have hit me earlier? Was I the victim of some crime?

And what happened between me and Gat? Did we argue? Did I wrong him?

Did he stop loving me and go back to Raquel?

I resolve that everything I learn in the next four weeks will go above my Windemere bed. I will sleep beneath the notes and study them every morning.

Maybe a picture will emerge from the pixels.

A WITCH HAS been standing there behind me for some time, waiting for a moment of weakness. She holds an ivory statue of a goose. It is intricately carved. I turn and admire it only for a moment before she swings it with shocking force. It connects, crushing a hole in my forehead. I can feel my bone come loose. The witch swings the statue again and hits above my right ear, smashing my skull. Blow after blow she lands, until tiny flakes of bone litter the bed and mingle with chipped bits of her once-beautiful goose.

I find my pills and turn off the light.

"Cadence?" Mummy calls from the hallway. "Supper is on at New Clairmont."

I can't go.

I can't. I won't.

Mummy promises coffee to help me stay awake while the drugs are in my system. She says how long it's been since the aunts have seen me, how the littles are my cousins, too, after all. I have family obligations.

I can only feel the break in my skull and the pain winging through my brain. Everything else is a faded backdrop to that.

Finally she leaves without me.

29

DEEP IN THE night, the house rattles—just the thing Taft was scared of over at Cuddledown. All the houses here do it. They're old, and the island is buffeted by winds off the sea.

I try to go back to sleep.

No.

I go downstairs and onto the porch. My head feels okay now.

Aunt Carrie is on the walkway, heading away from me in her nightgown and a pair of shearling boots. She looks skinny, with the bones of her chest exposed and her cheekbones hollow.

She turns onto the wooden walkway that leads to Red Gate.

I sit, staring after her. Breathing the night air and listening to the waves. A few minutes later she comes up the path from Cuddledown again.

"Cady," she says, stopping and crossing her arms over her chest. "You feeling better?"

"Sorry I missed supper," I say. "I had a headache."

"There will be suppers every night, all summer."

"Can't you sleep?"

"Oh, you know." Carrie scratches her neck. "I can't sleep without Ed. Isn't that silly?"

"No."

"I start wandering. It's good exercise. Have you seen Johnny?"

"Not in the middle of the night."

"He's up when I'm up, sometimes. Do you see him?"

"You could look if his light is on."

"Will has such bad nightmares," Carrie says. "He wakes up screaming and then I can't go back to sleep."

I shiver in my sweatshirt. "Do you want a flashlight?" I ask. "There's one inside the door."

"Oh, no. I like the dark."

She trudges once again up the hill.

30

MUMMY IS IN the New Clairmont kitchen with Granddad. I see them through the glass sliding doors.

"You're up early," she says when I come in. "Feeling better?"

Granddad is wearing a plaid bathrobe. Mummy is in a sundress decorated with small pink lobsters. She is making espresso. "Do you want scones? The cook made bacon, too. They're both in the warming drawer." She walks across the kitchen and lets the dogs into the house. Bosh, Grendel, and Poppy wag their tails and drool. Mummy bends and wipes their paws with a wet cloth, then absentmindedly swipes the floor where their muddy paw prints were. They sit stupidly, sweetly.

"Where's Fatima?" I ask. "Where's Prince Philip?"

"They're gone," says Mummy.

"What?"

"Be nice to her," says Granddad. He turns to me. "They passed on a while back."

"Both of them?"

Granddad nods.

"I'm sorry." I sit next to him at the table. "Did they suffer?"

"Not for long."

Mummy brings a plate of raspberry scones and one of bacon to the table. I take a scone and spread butter and honey on it. "She used to be a little blond girl. A Sinclair through and through," Granddad complains to Mummy.

"We talked about my hair when you came to visit," I remind him. "I don't expect you to like it. Grandfathers never like hair dye."

"You're the parent. You should make Mirren change her hair back how it was," Granddad says to my mother. "What happened to the little blond girls who used to run around this place?"

Mummy sighs. "We grew up, Dad," she says. "We grew up."

31

GIVEAWAYS: CHILDHOOD ART, botanic prints.

I get my laundry basket from Windemere and head to Cuddledown. Mirren meets me on the porch, skipping around. "It's so amazing to be on the island!" she says. "I can't believe I'm here again!"

"You were here last summer."

"It wasn't the same. No summer idyll like we used to have. They were doing construction on New Clairmont. Everyone was acting miserable and I kept looking for you but you never came."

"I told you I was going to Europe."

"Oh, I know."

"I wrote you a lot," I say. It comes out reproachful.

"I hate email!" says Mirren. "I read them all, but you can't be mad at me for not answering. It feels like homework, typing and staring at the stupid phone or the computer."

"Did you get the doll I sent you?"

Mirren puts her arms around me. "I missed you so much. You can't even believe how much."

"I sent you that Barbie. The one with the long hair we used to fight over."

"Princess Butterscotch?"

"Yeah."

"I was crazy about Princess Butterscotch."

"You hit me with her once."

"You deserved it!" Mirren jumps around happily. "Is she at Windemere?"

"What? No. I sent her in the mail," I say. "Over the winter."

Mirren looks at me, her brows furrowed. "I never got her, Cadence."

"Someone signed for the package. What did your mom do, shove it in a closet without opening it?"

I'm joking, but Mirren nods. "Maybe. She's compulsive. Like, she scrubs her hands over and over. Makes Taft and the twins do it, too. Cleans like there's a special place in heaven for people with spotless kitchen floors. Also she drinks too much."

"Mummy does, too."

Mirren nods. "I can't stand to watch."

"Did I miss anything at supper last night?"

"I didn't go." Mirren heads onto the wooden walkway that leads from Cuddledown to the tiny beach. I follow. "I told you I wasn't going this summer. Why didn't you come over here?"

"I got sick."

"We all know about your migraines," says Mirren. "The aunts have been talking."

I flinch. "Don't feel sorry for me, okay? Not ever. It makes my skin crawl."

"Didn't you take your pills last night?"

"They knocked me out."

We have reached the tiny beach. Both of us go barefoot across the damp sand. Mirren touches the shell of a long-dead crab.

I want to tell her that my memory is hacked, that I have a traumatic brain injury. I want to ask her everything that happened summer fifteen, make her tell me the stories Mummy doesn't want to talk about or doesn't know. But there is Mirren, so bright. I don't want her to feel more pity for me than she already does.

Also, I am still mad about the emails she didn't answer— and the loss of the stupid Barbie, though I'm sure it's not her fault.

"Are Johnny and Gat at Red Gate or did they sleep at Cuddledown?" I ask.

"Cuddledown. God, they're slobs. It's like living with goblins."

"Make them move back to Red Gate, then."

"No way," laughs Mirren. "And you—no more Windemere, okay? You'll move in with us?"

I shake my head. "Mummy says no. I asked her this morning."

"Come on, she has to let you!"

"She's all over me since I got sick."

"But that's nearly two years."

"Yeah. She watches me sleep. Plus she lectured me about bonding with Granddad and the littles. I have to connect with the family. Put on a smile."

"That's such bullshit." Mirren shows me a handful of tiny purple rocks she's collected. "Here."

"No, thanks." I don't want anything I don't need.

"Please take them," says Mirren. "I remember how you used to always search for purple rocks when we were little." She holds her hand out to me, palm up. "I want to make up for Princess Butterscotch." There are tears in her eyes. "And the emails," she adds. "I want to give you something, Cady."

"Okay, then," I say. I cup my hands and let Mirren pour the rocks into my palms. I store them in the front pocket of my hoodie.

"I love you!" she shouts. Then she turns and calls out to the sea. "I love my cousin Cadence Sinclair Eastman!"

"Overdoing it much?" It is Johnny, padding down the steps with bare feet, dressed in old flannel pajamas with a ticking stripe. He's wearing wraparound sunglasses and white sunblock down his nose like a lifeguard.

Mirren's face falls, but only momentarily. "I am expressing my feelings, Johnny. That is what being a living, breathing human being is all about. Hello?"

"Okay, living, breathing human being," he says, biffing her lightly on the shoulder. "But there's no need to do it so loudly at the crack of dawn. We have the whole summer in front of us."

She sticks out her bottom lip. "Cady's only here four weeks."

"I can't get ugly with you this early," says Johnny. "I haven't had my pretentious tea yet." He bends and looks in the laundry basket at my feet. "What's in here?"

"Botanic prints. And some of my old art."

"How come?" Johnny sits on a rock and I settle next to him.

"I am giving away my things," I say. "Since September. Remember I sent you the stripy scarf?"

"Oh, yeah."

I tell about giving the things to people who can use them, finding the right homes for them. I talk about charity and questioning Mummy's materialism.

I want Johnny and Mirren to understand me. I am not someone to pity, with an unstable mind and weird pain syndromes. I am taking charge of my life. I live according to my principles. I take action and make sacrifices.

"You don't, I dunno, want to own stuff?" Johnny asks me.

"Like what?"

"Oh, I want stuff all the time," says Johnny, throwing his arms wide. "A car. Video games. Expensive wool coats. I like watches, they're so old-school. I want real art for my walls, paintings by famous people I could never own in a million years. Fancy cakes I see in bakery windows. Sweaters, scarves. Wooly items with stripes, generally."

"Or you could want beautiful drawings you made when you were a kid," says Mirren, kneeling by the laundry basket. "Sentimental stuff." She picks up the crayon drawing of Gran with the goldens. "Look, this one is Fatima and this one is Prince Philip."

"You can tell?"

"Of course. Fatima had that chubby nose and wide face."

"God, Mirren. You're such a mushball," Johnny says.

32

GAT CALLS MY name as I am heading up the walkway to New Clairmont. I turn and he's running at me, wearing blue pajama pants and no shirt.

Gat. My Gat.

Is he going to be my Gat?

He stops in front of me, breathing hard. His hair sticks up, bedhead. The muscles of his abdomen ripple and he seems much more naked than he would in a swimsuit.

"Johnny said you were down at the tiny beach," he pants. "I looked for you there first."

"Did you just wake up?"

He rubs the back of his neck. Looks down at what he's wearing. "Kind of. I wanted to catch you."

"How come?"

"Let's go to the perimeter."

We head there and walk the way we did as children, Gat in front and me behind. We crest a low hill, then curve back behind the staff building to where the Vineyard harbor comes into view near the boathouse.

Gat turns so suddenly I nearly run into him, and before I can step back his arms are around me. He pulls me to his chest and buries his face in my neck. I wrap my bare arms around his torso, the insides of my wrists against his spine. He is warm.

"I didn't get to hug you yesterday," Gat whispers. "Everyone hugged you but me."

Touching him is familiar and unfamiliar.

We have been here before.

Also we have never been here before.

For a moment,

or for minutes,

for hours, possibly,

I am simply happy, here with Gat's body beneath my hands. The sound of the waves and his breath in my ear. Glad that he wants to be near me.

"Do you remember when we came down here together?" he asks into my neck. "The time we went out on that flat rock?"

I step away. Because I don't remember.

I hate my fucking hacked-up mind, how sick I am all the time, how damaged I've become. I hate that I've lost my looks and failed school and quit sports and am cruel to my mother. I hate how I still want him after two years.

Maybe Gat wants to be with me. Maybe. But more likely he's just looking for me to tell him he did nothing wrong when he left me two summers ago. He'd like me to tell him I'm not mad. That he's a great guy.

But how can I forgive him when I don't even know exactly what he's done to me?

"No," I answer. "It must have slipped my mind."

"We were— You and I, we— It was an important moment."

"Whatever," I say. "I don't remember it. And obviously nothing that happened between us was particularly important in the long run, was it?"

He looks at his hands. "Okay. Sorry. That was extremely suboptimal of me just now. Are you angry?"

"Of course I'm angry," I say. "Two years of disappearance. Never calling and not writing back and making everything worse by not dealing. Now you're all, *Ooh, I thought I'd never see you again*, and holding my hand and *Everyone hugs you but me* and half-naked perimeter walking. It's severely *suboptimal*, Gat. If that's the word you want to use."

His face falls. "It sounds awful when you put it that way."

"Yeah, well, that's how I see it."

He rubs his hand on his hair. "I'm handling everything badly," he says. "What would you say if I asked you to start over?"

"God, Gat."

"What?"

"Just *ask*. Don't ask what I'd say if you *did* ask."

"Okay, I'm asking. Can we start over? Please, Cady? Let's start over after lunch. It'll be awesome. I'll make amusing remarks and you'll laugh. We'll go troll hunting. We'll be happy to see each other. You'll think I'm great, I promise."

"That's a big promise."

"Okay, maybe not great, but at least I won't be suboptimal."

"Why say suboptimal? Why not say what you really are? Thoughtless and confusing and manipulative?"

"God." Gat jumps up and down in agitation. "Cadence! I really need to just start over. This is going from suboptimal down to total crap." He jumps and kicks his legs out like an angry little boy.

The jumping makes me smile. "Okay," I tell him. "Start over. After lunch."

"All right," he says, and stops jumping. "After lunch."

We stare at each other for a moment.

"I'm going to run away now," says Gat. "Don't take it personally."

"Okay."

"It's better for the starting over if I run. Because walking will just be awkward."

"I said okay."

"Okay, then."

And he runs.

33

I GO TO lunch at New Clairmont an hour later. I know Mummy will not tolerate my absence after I missed supper last night. Granddad gives me a tour of the house while the cook sets out food and the aunts corral the littles.

It's a sharp place. Shining wood floors, huge windows, everything low to the ground. The halls of Clairmont used to be decorated floor to ceiling with black-and-white family photographs, paintings of dogs, bookshelves, and Granddad's collection of *New Yorker* cartoons. New Clairmont's halls are glass on one side and blank on the other.

Granddad opens the doors to the four guest bedrooms upstairs. All are furnished only with beds and low, wide dressers. The windows have white shades that let some light shine in. There are no patterns on the bedspreads; they are simple, tasteful shades of blue or brown.

The littles' rooms have some life. Taft has a Bakugan arena on the floor, a soccer ball, books about wizards and orphans. Liberty and Bonnie brought magazines and an MP3 player. They have stacks of Bonnie's books on ghost hunters, psychics, and dangerous angels. Their dresser is cluttered with makeup and perfume bottles. Tennis racquets in the corner.

Granddad's bedroom is larger than the others and has the best view. He takes me in and shows me the bathroom, which has handles in the shower. Old-person handles, so he won't fall down.

"Where are your *New Yorker* cartoons?" I ask.

"The decorator made decisions."

"What about the pillows?"

"The what?"

"You had all those pillows. With embroidered dogs."

He shakes his head.

"Did you keep the fish?"

"What, the swordfish and all that?" We walk down the staircase to the ground floor. Granddad moves slowly and I am behind him. "I started over with this house," he says simply. "That old life is gone."

He opens the door to his study. It's as severe as the rest of the house. A laptop sits in the center of a large desk. A large window looks out over the Japanese garden. A chair. A wall of shelves, completely empty.

It feels clean and open, but it isn't spartan, because every-thing is opulent.

Granddad is more like Mummy than like me. He's erased his old life by spending money on a replacement one.

"Where's the young man?" asks Granddad suddenly. His face takes on a vacant look.

"Johnny?"

He shakes his head. "No, no."

"Gat?"

"Yes, the young man." He clutches the desk for a moment, as if feeling faint.

"Granddad, are you okay?"

"Oh, fine."

"Gat is at Cuddledown with Mirren and Johnny," I tell him.

"There was a book I promised him."

"Most of your books aren't here."

"Stop telling me what's not here!" Granddad yells, suddenly forceful.

"You okay?" It is Aunt Carrie, standing in the door of the study.

"I'm all right," he says.

Carrie gives me a look and takes Granddad's arm. "Come on. Lunch is ready."

"Did you get back to sleep?" I ask my aunt as we head toward the kitchen. "Last night, was Johnny up?"

"I don't know what you're talking about," she says.

34

GRANDDAD'S COOK DOES the shopping and preps the meals, but the aunties plan all the menus. Today we have cold roast chicken, tomato-basil salad, Camembert, baguettes, and strawberry lemonade in the dining room. Liberty shows me pictures of cute boys in a magazine. Then she shows me pictures of clothes in another magazine. Bonnie reads a book called *Collective Apparitions: Fact and Fiction*. Taft and Will want me to take them tubing—drive the small motorboat while they float behind it in an inner tube.

Mummy says I'm not allowed to drive the boat on meds.

Aunt Carrie says that doesn't matter, because no way is Will going tubing.

Aunt Bess says she agrees, so Taft better not even think about asking her.

Liberty and Bonnie ask if they can go tubing. "You always let Mirren go," says Liberty. "You know it's true."

Will spills his lemonade and soaks a baguette.

Granddad's lap gets wet.

Taft gets hold of the wet baguette and hits Will with it.

Mummy wipes the mess while Bess runs upstairs to bring Granddad clean trousers.

Carrie scolds the boys.

When the meal is over, Taft and Will duck into the living room to avoid helping with the cleanup. They jump like lunatics on Granddad's new leather couch. I follow.

Will is runty and pink, like Johnny. Hair almost white. Taft is taller and very thin, golden and freckled, with long dark lashes and a mouth full of braces. "So, you two," I say. "How was last summer?"

"Do you know how to get an ash dragon in *DragonVale*?" asks Will.

"I know how to get a scorch dragon," says Taft.

"You can use the scorch dragon to get the ash dragon," says Will.

Ugh. Ten-year-olds. "Come on. Last summer," I say. "Tell me. Did you play tennis?"

"Sure," says Will.

"Did you go swimming?"

"Yeah," says Taft.

"Did you go boating with Gat and Johnny?"

They both stop jumping. "No."

"Did Gat say anything about me?"

"I'm not supposed to talk about you ending up in the water and everything," says Will. "I promised Aunt Penny I wouldn't."

"Why not?" I ask.

"It'll make your headaches worse and we have to leave the subject alone."

Taft nods. "She said if we make your headaches worse she'll string us up by our toenails and take away the iPads. We're supposed to act cheerful and not be idiots."

"This isn't about my accident," I say. "This is about the summer when I went to Europe."

"Cady?" Taft touches my shoulder. "Bonnie saw pills in your bedroom."

Will backs away and sits on the far arm of the sofa.

"Bonnie went through my stuff?"

"And Liberty."

"God."

"You told me you weren't a drug addict, but you have pills on your dresser." Taft is petulant.

"Tell them to stay out of my room," I say.

"If you're a drug addict," says Taft, "there is something you need to know."

"What?"

"Drugs are not your friend." Taft looks serious. "Drugs are not your friend and also people should be your friends."

"Oh, my God. Would you just tell me what you did last summer, pipsqueak?"

Will says, "Taft and I want to play *Angry Birds*. We don't want to talk to you anymore."

"Whatever," I say. "Go and be free."

I step onto the porch and watch the boys as they run down the path to Red Gate.

35

ALL THE WINDOWS in Cuddledown are open when I come down after lunch. Gat is putting music on the ancient CD player. My old crayon art is on the refrigerator with magnets: Dad on top, Gran and the goldens on the bottom. My painting is taped to one of the kitchen cupboards. A ladder and a big box of gift wrap stand in the center of the great room.

Mirren pushes an armchair across the floor. "I never liked the way my mother kept this place," she explains.

I help Gat and Johnny move the furniture around until Mirren is happy. We take down Bess's landscape watercolors and roll up her rugs. We pillage the littles' bedrooms for fun objects. When we are done, the great room is decorated with piggy banks and patchwork quilts, stacks of children's books, a lamp shaped like an owl. Thick sparkling ribbons from the gift-wrap box crisscross the ceiling.

"Won't Bess be mad you're redecorating?" I ask.

"I promise you she's not setting foot in Cuddledown for the rest of the summer. She's been trying to get out of this place for years."

"What do you mean?"

"Oh," says Mirren lightly, "you know. Natter natter, least favorite daughter, natter natter, the kitchen is such crap. Why won't Granddad remodel it? Et cetera."

"Did she ask him?"

Johnny stares at me oddly. "You don't remember?"

"Her memory is messed up, Johnny!" yells Mirren. "She doesn't remember like half our summer fifteen."

"She doesn't?" Johnny says. "I thought—"

"No, no, shut up right now," Mirren barks. "Did you not listen to what I told you?"

"When?" He looks perplexed.

"The other night," says Mirren. "I told you what Aunt Penny said."

"Chill," says Johnny, throwing a pillow at her.

"This is important! How can you not pay attention to this stuff?" Mirren looks like she might cry.

"I'm sorry, all right?" Johnny says. "Gat, did you know about Cadence not remembering, like, most of the summer fifteen?"

"I knew," he says.

"See?" says Mirren. "Gat was listening."

My face is hot. I am looking at the floor. No one speaks for a minute. "It's normal to lose some memory when you hit your head really hard," I say finally. "Did my mother explain?"

Johnny laughs nervously.

"I'm surprised Mummy told you," I go on. "She hates talking about it."

"She said you're supposed to take it easy and remember things in your own time. All the aunties know," says Mirren. "Granddad knows. The littles. The staff. Every single person on the island knows but Johnny, apparently."

"I knew," says Johnny. "I just didn't know the whole picture."

"Don't be feeble," says Mirren. "Now is really not the time."

"It's okay," I say to Johnny. "You're not feeble. You merely had a suboptimal moment. I'm sure you'll be optimal from now on."

"I'm always optimal," says Johnny. "Just not the kind of optimal Mirren wants me to be."

Gat smiles when I say the word *suboptimal* and pats my shoulder.

We have started over.

36

WE PLAY TENNIS. Johnny and I win, but not because I'm any good anymore. He's an excellent athlete, and Mirren is more inclined to hit the ball and then do happy dances, without caring whether it's returning. Gat keeps laughing at her, which makes him miss.

"How was Europe?" asks Gat as we walk back to Cuddledown.

"My father ate squid ink."

"What else?" We reach the yard and toss the racquets on the porch. Stretch ourselves out on the grass.

"Honestly, I can't tell you that much," I say. "Know what I did while my dad went to the Colosseum?"

"What?"

"I lay with my face pressed into the tile of the hotel bathroom. Stared at the base of the blue Italian toilet."

"The toilet was blue?" Johnny asks, sitting up.

"Only *you* would get more excited over a blue toilet than the sights of Rome," moans Gat.

"Cadence," says Mirren.

"What?"

"Never mind."

"What?"

"You say don't feel sorry for you, but then you tell a story about the base of the toilet," she blurts. "It's seriously pitiful. What are we supposed to say?"

"Also, going to Rome makes us jealous," says Gat. "None of us has been to Rome."

"I want to go to Rome!" says Johnny, lying back down. "I want to see the blue Italian toilets so bad!"

"I want to see the Baths of Caracalla," says Gat. "And eat every flavor of gelato they make."

"So go," I say.

"It's hardly that simple."

"Okay, but you will go," I say. "In college or after college."

Gat sighs. "I'm just saying, you went to Rome."

"I wish you could have been there," I tell him.

37

"WERE YOU ON the tennis court?" Mummy asks me. "I heard balls."

"Just messing around."

"You haven't played in so long. That's wonderful."

"My serve is off."

96

"I'm so happy you're taking it up again. If you want to hit with me tomorrow, say the word."

She is delusional. I am not taking up tennis again just because I played one single afternoon, and in no capacity do I ever want to hit with Mummy. She will wear a tennis skirt and praise me and caution me and hover over me until I'm unkind to her. "We'll see," I say. "I probably strained my shoulder."

Supper is outside in the Japanese garden. We watch the eight o'clock sunset, in groups around the small tables. Taft and Will grab pork chops off the platter and eat them with their hands.

"You two are animals," says Liberty, wrinkling her nose.

"And your point is?" says Taft.

"There's a thing called a fork," says Liberty.

"There's a thing called your face," says Taft.

Johnny, Gat, and Mirren get to eat at Cuddledown because they aren't invalids. And their mothers aren't controlling. Mummy doesn't even let me sit with the adults. She makes me sit at a separate table with my cousins.

They're all laughing and sniping at each other, talking with their mouths full. I stop listening to what they are saying. Instead, I look across to Mummy, Carrie, and Bess, clustered around Granddad.

THERE'S A NIGHT I remember now. It must have been about two weeks before my accident. Early July. We were all sitting at the long table on the Clairmont lawn. Citronella candles burned on the porch. The littles had finished their burgers and were doing cartwheels on the grass. The rest of us were eating grilled swordfish with basil sauce. There was a salad of yellow tomatoes and a casserole of zucchini with a crust of Parmesan cheese. Gat pressed his leg against mine under the table. I felt light-headed with happiness.

The aunts toyed with their food, silent and formal with one another beneath the littles' shouts. Granddad leaned back, folding his hands over his abdomen. "You think I should renovate the Boston house?" he asked.

A silence followed.

"No, Dad." Bess was the first to speak. "We love that house."

"You always complain about drafts in the living room," said Granddad.

Bess looked around at her sisters. "I don't."

"You don't like the décor," said Granddad.

"That's true." Mummy's voice was critical.

"I think it's timeless," said Carrie.

"I could use your advice, you know," Granddad said to Bess. "Would you come over and look at it carefully? Tell me what you think?"

"I . . ."

He leaned in. "I could sell it, too, you know."

We all knew Aunt Bess wanted the Boston house. All the aunts wanted the Boston house. It was a four-million-dollar house, and they grew up in it. But Bess was the only one who lived nearby, and the only one with enough kids to fill the bedrooms.

"Dad," Carrie said sharply. "You can't sell it."

"I can do what I want," said Granddad, spearing the last tomato on his plate and popping it in his mouth. "You like the house as it is, then, Bess? Or do you want to see it remodeled? No one likes a waffler."

"I'd love to help with whatever you want to change, Dad."

"Oh, please," snapped Mummy. "Only yesterday you were

saying how busy you are and now you're helping remodel the Boston house?"

"He asked for our help," said Bess.

"He asked for *your* help. You cutting us out, Dad?" Mummy was drunk.

Granddad laughed. "Penny, relax."

"I'll relax when the estate is settled."

"You're making us crazy," Carrie muttered.

"What was that? Don't mumble."

"We all love you, Dad," said Carrie, loudly. "I know it's been hard this year."

"If you're going crazy it's your own damn choice," said Granddad. "Pull yourself together. I can't leave the estate to crazy people."

LOOK AT THE aunties now, summer seventeen. Here in the Japanese garden of New Clairmont, Mummy has her arm around Bess, who reaches out to slice Carrie a piece of rasp-berry tart.

It's a beautiful night, and we are indeed a beautiful family.

I do not know what changed.

38

"TAFT HAS A motto," I tell Mirren. It is midnight. We Liars are playing Scrabble in the Cuddledown great room.

My knee is touching Gat's thigh, though I am not sure he

notices. The board is nearly full. My brain is tired. I have bad letters.

Mirren rearranges her tiles distractedly. "Taft has what?"

"A motto," I say. "You know, like Granddad has? No one likes a waffler?"

"Never take a seat in the back of the room," intones Mirren.

"Never complain, never explain," says Gat. "That's from Disraeli, I think."

"Oh, he loves that one," says Mirren.

"And don't take no for an answer," I add.

"Good lord, Cady!" shouts Johnny. "Will you just build a word and let the rest of us get on with it?"

"Don't yell at her, Johnny," says Mirren.

"Sorry," says Johnny. "Will you pretty please with brown sugar and cinnamon make a fucking Scrabble word?"

My knee is touching Gat's thigh. I really can't think. I make a short, lame word.

Johnny plays his tiles.

"Drugs are not your friend," I announce. "That's Taft's motto."

"Get out," laughs Mirren. "Where did he come up with that?"

"Maybe he had drug education at school. Plus the twins snooped in my room and told him I had a dresser full of pills, so he wanted to make sure I'm not an addict."

"God," said Mirren. "Bonnie and Liberty are disasters. I think they're kleptomaniacs now."

"Really?"

"They took my mom's sleeping pills and also her diamond hoops. I have no idea where they think they'll wear those earrings where she wouldn't see them. Also, they are two people and it's only one pair."

"Did you call them on it?"

"I tried with Bonnie. But they're beyond my help," Mirren says. She rearranges her tiles again. "I like the idea of a motto," she goes on. "I think an inspirational quote can get you through hard times."

"Like what?" asks Gat.

Mirren pauses. Then she says: "Be a little kinder than you have to."

We are all silenced by that. It seems impossible to argue with.

Then Johnny says, "Never eat anything bigger than your ass."

"You ate something bigger than your ass?" I ask.

He nods, solemn.

"Okay, Gat," says Mirren. "What's yours?"

"Don't have one."

"Come on."

"Okay, maybe." Gat looks down at his fingernails. "Do not accept an evil you can change."

"I agree with that," I say. Because I do.

"I don't," says Mirren.

"Why not?"

"There's very little you can change. You need to accept the world as it is."

"Not true," says Gat.

"Isn't it better to be a relaxed, peaceful person?" Mirren asks.

"No." Gat is decisive. "It is better to fight evil."

"Don't eat yellow snow," says Johnny. "That's another good motto."

"Always do what you are afraid to do," I say. "That's mine."

"Oh, please. Who the hell says that?" barks Mirren.

"Emerson," I answer. "I think." I reach for a pen and write it on the backs of my hands.

Left: *Always do what.* Right: *you are afraid to do.* The handwriting is skewed on the right.

"Emerson is so boring," says Johnny. He grabs the pen from me and writes on his own left hand: NO YELLOW SNOW. "There," he says, holding the result up for display. "That should help."

"Cady, I'm serious. We should *not* always do what we are afraid to do," says Mirren heatedly. "We never should."

"Why not?"

"You could die. You could get hurt. If you are terrified, there's probably a good reason. You should trust your impulses."

"So what's your philosophy, then?" Johnny asks her. "Be a giant chickenhead?"

"Yes," says Mirren. "That and the kindness thing I said before."

39

I FOLLOW GAT when he goes upstairs. I chase after him down the long hall, grab his hand and pull his lips to mine.

It is what I am afraid to do, and I do it.

He kisses me back. His fingers twine in mine and I'm dizzy

and he's holding me up and everything is clear and everything is grand, again. Our kiss turns the world to dust. There is only us and nothing else matters.

Then Gat pulls away. "I shouldn't do this."

"Why not?" His hand still holds mine.

"It's not that I don't want to, it's—"

"I thought we started over. Isn't this the starting over?"

"I'm a mess." Gat steps back and leans against the wall. "This is such a cliché conversation. I don't know what else to say."

"Explain."

A pause. And then: "You don't know me."

"Explain," I say again.

Gat puts his head in his hands. We stand there, both leaning against the wall in the dark. "Okay. Here's part of it," he finally whispers. "You've never met my mom. You've never been to my apartment."

That's true. I've never seen Gat anywhere but Beechwood.

"You feel like you know me, Cady, but you only know the me who comes here," he says. "It's—it's just not the whole picture. You don't know my bedroom with the window onto the airshaft, my mom's curry, the guys from school, the way we celebrate holidays. You only know the me on this island, where everyone's rich except me and the staff. Where everyone's white except me, Ginny, and Paulo."

"Who are Ginny and Paulo?"

Gat hits his fist into his palm. "Ginny is the housekeeper. Paulo is the gardener. You don't know their names and they've worked here summer after summer. That's part of my point."

My face heats with shame. "I'm sorry."

"But do you even want to see the whole picture?" Gat asks. "Could you even understand it?"

"You won't know unless you try me," I say. "I haven't heard from you in forever."

"You know what I am to your grandfather? What I've always been?"

"What?"

"Heathcliff. In *Wuthering Heights*. Have you read it?"

I shake my head.

"Heathcliff is a gypsy boy taken in and raised by this pristine family, the Earnshaws. Heathcliff falls in love with the girl, Catherine. She loves him, too—but she also thinks he's dirt, because of his background. And the rest of the family agrees."

"That's not how I feel."

"There's nothing Heathcliff can ever do to make these Earnshaws think he's good enough. And he tries. He goes away, educates himself, becomes a gentleman. Still, they think he's an animal."

"And?"

"Then, because the book is a tragedy, Heathcliff becomes what they think of him, you know? He becomes a brute. The evil in him comes out."

"I heard it was a romance."

Gat shakes his head. "Those people are awful to each other."

"You're saying Granddad thinks you're Heathcliff?"

"I promise you, he does," says Gat. "A brute beneath a pleasant surface, betraying his kindness in letting me come to his sheltered island every year—I've betrayed him by seducing his Catherine, his Cadence. And my penance is to become the monster he always saw in me."

I am silent.

Gat is silent.

I reach out and touch him. Just the feel of his forearm beneath the thin cotton of his shirt makes me ache to kiss him again.

"You know what's terrifying?" Gat says, not looking at me. "What's terrifying is he's turned out to be right."

"No, he hasn't."

"Oh, yes, he has."

"Gat, wait."

But he has gone into his room and shut the door.

I am alone in the dark hallway.

40

ONCE UPON A time, there was a king who had three beautiful daughters. The girls grew up as lovely as the day was long. They made grand marriages, too, but the arrival of the first grandchild brought disappointment. The youngest princess produced a daughter so very, very tiny that her mother took to keeping her in a pocket, where the girl went unnoticed. Eventually, normal-sized grandchildren arrived, and the king and queen forgot the existence of the tiny princess almost completely.

When the too-small princess grew older, she passed most of her days and nights hardly ever leaving her tiny bed. There was very little reason for her to get up, so solitary was she.

One day, she ventured to the palace library and was delighted to find what good company books could be. She began going there often. One morning, as she read, a mouse appeared on the table. He stood upright and wore a small velvet jacket. His whiskers were clean and his fur was brown. "You read just as I do," he said, "walking back and forth across the pages." He stepped forward and made a low bow.

The mouse charmed the tiny princess with stories of his adventures. He told her of trolls who steal people's feet and gods who abandon the poor. He asked questions about the universe and searched continually for answers. He thought wounds needed attention. In turn, the princess told the mouse fairy tales, drew him pixelated portraits, and made him little crayon drawings. She laughed and argued with him. She felt awake for the first time in her life.

It was not long before they loved each other dearly.

When she presented her suitor to her family, however, the princess met with difficulty. "He is only a mouse!" cried the king in disdain, while the queen screamed and ran from the throne room in fear. Indeed, the entire kingdom, from royalty to servants, viewed the mouse suitor with suspicion and discomfort. "He is unnatural," people said of him. "An animal masquerading as a person."

The tiny princess did not hesitate. She and the mouse left the palace and traveled far, far away. In a foreign land they were married, made a home for themselves, filled it with books and chocolate, and lived happily ever after.

If you want to live where people are not afraid of mice, you must give up living in palaces.

41

A GIANT WIELDS a rusty saw. He gloats and hums as he works, slicing through my forehead and into the mind behind it.

I have less than four weeks to find out the truth.

Granddad calls me Mirren.

The twins are stealing sleeping pills and diamond earrings.

Mummy argued with the aunts over the Boston house.

Bess hates Cuddledown.

Carrie roams the island at night.

Will has bad dreams.

Gat is Heathcliff.

Gat thinks I do not know him.

And maybe he is right.

I take pills. Drink water. The room is dark.

Mummy stands in the doorway, watching me. I do not speak to her.

I am in bed for two days. Every now and then the sharp pain wanes to an ache. Then, if I am alone, I sit up and write on the cluster of notes above my bed. Questions more than answers.

The morning I feel better, Granddad comes over to Windemere early. He's wearing white linen pants and a blue sport jacket. I am in shorts and a T-shirt, throwing balls for the dogs in the yard. Mummy is already up at New Clairmont.

"I'm heading to Edgartown," Granddad says, scratching

Bosh's ears. "You want to come? If you don't mind an old man's company."

"I don't know," I joke. "I'm so busy with these spit-covered tennis balls. Could be all day."

"I'll take you to the bookstore, Cady. Buy you presents like I used to."

"How about fudge?"

Granddad laughs. "Sure, fudge."

"Did Mummy put you up to this?"

"No." He scratches his tufty white hair. "But Bess doesn't want me driving the motorboat alone. She says I could get disoriented."

"I'm not allowed to drive the motorboat, either."

"I know," he says, holding up the keys. "But Bess and Penny aren't boss here. I am."

We decide to eat breakfast in town. We want to get the boat away from the Beechwood dock before the aunts catch us.

EDGARTOWN IS A nautical, sweetie-pie village on Martha's Vineyard. It takes twenty minutes to get there. It's all white picket fences and white wooden homes with flowery yards. Shops sell tourist stuff, ice cream, pricey clothes, antique jewelry. Boats leave from the harbor for fishing trips and scenic cruises.

Granddad seems like his old self. He's tossing money around. Treats me to espresso and croissants at a little bakery with stools by a window, then tries to buy me books at the Edgartown bookshop. When I refuse the gift, he shakes his head at my giveaway project but doesn't lecture. Instead he asks for my help picking out presents for the littles and a floral design book for Ginny, the housekeeper. We place a big order at Murdick's Fudge: chocolate, chocolate walnut, peanut butter, and penuche.

Browsing in one of the art galleries, we run into Granddad's lawyer, a narrow, graying fellow named Richard Thatcher. "So this is Cadence the first," says Thatcher, shaking my hand. "I've heard a great deal about you."

"He does the estate," says Granddad, by way of explanation.

"First grandchild," says Thatcher. "There's never anything to match that feeling."

"She's got a great head on her shoulders, too," Granddad says. "Sinclair blood through and through."

This speaking in stock phrases, he has always done it. "Never complain, never explain." "Don't take no for an answer." But it grates when he's using them about me. A good head on my shoulders? My actual head is fucking broken in countless medically diagnosed ways—and half of me comes from the unfaithful Eastman side of the family. I am not going to college next year; I've given up all the sports I used to do and clubs I used to be part of; I'm high on Percocet half the time and I'm not even nice to my little cousins.

Still, Granddad's face is glowing as he talks about me, and at least today he knows I am not Mirren.

"She looks like you," says Thatcher.

"Doesn't she? Except she's good-looking."

"Thank you," I say. "But if you want the full resemblance I have to tuft up my hair."

This makes Granddad smile. "It's from the boat," he says to Thatcher. "Didn't bring a hat."

"It's always tufty," I tell Thatcher.

"I know," he says.

The men shake hands and Granddad hooks his arm through mine as we leave the gallery. "He's taken good care of you," he tells me.

"Mr. Thatcher?"

He nods. "But don't tell your mother. She'll stir up trouble again."

42

ON THE WAY home, a memory comes.

Summer fifteen, a morning in early July. Granddad was making espresso in the Clairmont kitchen. I was eating jam and baguette toast at the table. It was just the two of us.

"I love that goose," I said, pointing. A cream goose statue sat on the sideboard.

"It's been there since you, Johnny, and Mirren were three," said Granddad. "That's the year Tipper and I took that trip to China." He chuckled. "She bought a lot of art there. We had a guide, an art specialist." He came over to the toaster and popped the piece of bread I had in there for myself.

"Hey!" I objected.

"Shush, I'm the granddad. I can take the toast when I want to." He sat down with his espresso and spread butter on the baguette. "This art specialist girl took us to antiques shops and helped us navigate the auction houses," he said. "She spoke four languages. You wouldn't think to look at her. Little slip of a China girl."

"Don't say *China girl*. Hello?"

He ignored me. "Tipper bought jewelry and had the idea of buying animal sculptures for the houses here."

"Does that include the toad in Cuddledown?"

"Sure, the ivory toad," said Granddad. "And we bought two elephants, I know."

"Those are in Windemere."

"And monkeys in Red Gate. There were four monkeys."

"Isn't ivory illegal?" I asked.

"Oh, some places. But you can get it. Your gran loved ivory. She traveled to China when she was a child."

"Is it elephant tusks?"

"That or rhino."

There he was, Granddad. His white hair still thick, the lines on his face deep from all those days on the sailboat. His heavy jaw like an old film star.

You can get it, he said, about the ivory.

One of his mottos: Don't take no for an answer.

It had always seemed a heroic way to live. He would say it when advising us to pursue our ambitions. When encouraging Johnny to try training for a marathon, or when I failed to win the reading prize in seventh grade. It was something he said when talking about his business strategies, and how he got Gran to marry him. "I asked her four times before she said yes," he'd always say, retelling one of his favorite Sinclair family legends. "I wore her down. She said yes to shut me up."

Now, at the breakfast table, watching him eat my toast, "Don't take no for an answer" seemed like the attitude of a privileged guy who didn't care who got hurt, so long as his wife had the cute statues she wanted to display in her summer-houses.

I walked over and picked up the goose. "People shouldn't

buy ivory," I said. "It's illegal for a reason. Gat was reading the other day about—"

"Don't tell me what that boy is reading," snapped Granddad. "I'm informed. I get all the papers."

"Sorry. But he's made me think about—"

"Cadence."

"You could put the statues up for auction and then donate the money to wildlife conservation."

"Then I wouldn't have the statues. They were very dear to Tipper."

"But—"

Granddad barked, "Do not tell me what to do with my money, Cady. That money is not yours."

"Okay."

"You are not to tell me how to dispose of what is mine, is that clear?"

"Yes."

"Not ever."

"Yes, Granddad."

I had the urge to snatch the goose and fling it across the room.

Would it break when it hit the fireplace? Would it shatter?

I balled my hands into fists.

It was the first time we'd talked about Granny Tipper since her death.

GRANDDAD DOCKS THE boat and ties it up.

"Do you still miss Gran?" I ask him as we head toward New Clairmont. "Because I miss her. We never talk about her."

"A part of me died," he says. "And it was the best part."

"You think so?" I ask.

"That is all there is to say about it," says Granddad.

43

I FIND THE Liars in the Cuddledown yard. The grass is littered with tennis racquets and drink bottles, food wrappers and beach towels. The three of them lie on cotton blankets, wearing sunglasses and eating potato chips.

"Feeling better?" asks Mirren.

I nod.

"We missed you."

They have baby oil spread on their bodies. Two bottles of it lie on the grass. "Aren't you afraid you'll get burned?" I ask.

"I don't believe in sunblock anymore," says Johnny.

"He's decided the scientists are corrupt and the whole sunblock industry is a moneymaking fraud," says Mirren.

"Have you ever seen sun poisoning?" I ask. "The skin literally bubbles."

"It's a dumb idea," says Mirren. "We're just bored out of our minds, that's all." But she slathers baby oil on her arms as she's speaking.

I lie down next to Johnny.

I open a bag of barbeque potato chips.

I stare at Gat's chest.

Mirren reads aloud a bit of a book about Jane Goodall.

We listen to some music off my iPhone, the speaker tinny.

"Why don't you believe in sunblock again?" I ask Johnny.

"It's a conspiracy," he says. "To sell a lot of lotion that nobody needs."

"Uh-huh."

"I won't burn," he says. "You'll see."

"But why are you putting on baby oil?"

"Oh, that's not part of the experiment," Johnny says. "I just like to be as greasy as possible at all times."

GAT CATCHES ME in the kitchen, looking for food. There isn't much. "Last time I saw you was again suboptimal," he says. "In the hallway a couple nights ago."

"Yeah." My hands are shaking.

"Sorry."

"All right."

"Can we start over?"

"We can't start over every day, Gat."

"Why not?" He jumps to sit on the counter. "Maybe this is a summer of second chances."

"Second, sure. But after that it gets ridiculous."

"So just be normal," he says, "at least for today. Let's pretend I'm not a mess, let's pretend you're not angry. Let's act like we're friends and forget what happened."

I don't want to pretend.

I don't want to be friends.

I don't want to forget. I am trying to remember.

"Just for a day or two, until things start to seem all right again," says Gat, seeing my hesitation. "We'll just hang out until it all stops being such a big deal."

114

I want to know everything, understand everything; I want to hold Gat close and run my hands over him and never let him go. But perhaps this is the only way we can start.

Be normal, now. Right now.

Because you are. Because you can be.

"I've learned how to do that," I say.

I hand him the bag of fudge Granddad and I bought in Edgartown, and the way his face lights up at the chocolate tugs at my heart.

44

NEXT DAY MIRREN and I take the small motorboat to Edgartown without permission.

The boys don't want to come. They are going kayaking.

I drive and Mirren trails her hand in the wake.

Mirren isn't wearing much: a daisy-print bikini top and a denim miniskirt. She walks down the cobblestone sidewalks of Edgartown talking about Drake Loggerhead and how it feels to have "sexual intercourse" with him. That's what she calls it every time; her answer about how it feels has to do with the scent of beach roses mixed with roller coasters and fireworks.

She also talks about what clothes she wants to buy for freshman year at Pomona and movies she wants to see and projects she wants to do this summer, like find a place on the Vineyard to ride horses and start making ice cream again. Honestly, she doesn't stop chattering for half an hour.

I wish I had her life. A boyfriend, plans, college in California.

Mirren is going off into her sunshine future, whereas I am going back to Dickinson Academy to another year of snow and suffocation.

I buy a small bag of fudge at Murdick's, even though there's some left from yesterday. We sit on a shady bench, Mirren still talking.

Another memory comes.

SUMMER FIFTEEN, MIRREN sat next to Taft and Will on the steps of our favorite Edgartown clam shack. The boys had plastic rainbow pinwheels. Taft's face was smeared with fudge he'd eaten earlier. We were waiting for Bess, because she had Mirren's shoes. We couldn't go indoors without them.

Mirren's feet were dirty and her toenails painted blue.

We had been waiting a while when Gat came out of the shop down the block. He had a stack of books under his arm. He ran toward us at top speed, as if in a ridiculous hurry to catch us, even though we were sitting still.

Then he stopped short. The book on top was *Being and Nothingness* by Sartre. He still had the words written on the backs of his hands. A recommendation from Granddad.

Gat bowed, foolishly, clownishly, and presented me with the book at the bottom of the pile: it was a novel by Jaclyn Moriarty. I'd been reading her all summer.

I opened the book to the title page. It was inscribed. *For Cady with everything, everything. Gat.*

"I REMEMBER WAITING for your shoes so we could go into the clam shack," I tell Mirren. She has stopped talking now and looks at me expectantly. "Pinwheels," I say. "Gat giving me a book."

"So your memories are coming back," Mirren says. "That's great!"

"The aunties fought about the estate."

She shrugs. "A bit."

"And Granddad and I, we had this argument about his ivory statues."

"Yeah. We talked about it at the time."

"Tell me something."

"What?"

"Why did Gat disappear after my accident?"

Mirren twists a strand of her hair. "I don't know."

"Did he go back with Raquel?"

"I don't know."

"Did we fight? Did I do something wrong?"

"I don't know, Cady."

"He got upset at me a few nights back. About not knowing the names of the staff. About not having seen his apartment in New York."

There is a silence. "He has good reasons to be mad," says Mirren finally.

"What did I do?"

Mirren sighs. "You can't fix it."

"Why not?

Suddenly Mirren starts choking. Gagging, like she might vomit. Bending over at the waist, her skin damp and pale.

"You okay?"

"No."

"Can I help?"

She doesn't answer.

I offer her a bottle of water. She takes it. Drinks slowly. "I did too much. I need to get back to Cuddledown. Now."

Her eyes are glassy. I hold out my hand. Her skin feels wet and she seems unsteady on her feet. We walk in silence to the harbor where the small motorboat is docked.

MUMMY NEVER NOTICED the motorboat was missing, but she sees the bag of fudge when I give it to Taft and Will.

On and on, natter natter. Her lecture isn't interesting.

I may not leave the island without permission from her.

I may not leave the island without adult supervision.

I may not operate a motor vehicle on medication.

I can't be as stupid as I'm acting, can I?

I say the "Sorry" my mother wants to hear. Then I run down to Windemere and write everything I remembered—the clam shack, the pinwheel, Mirren's dirty feet on the wooden steps, the book Gat gave me—on the graph paper above my bed.

45

START OF MY second week on Beechwood, we discover the roof of Cuddledown. It's easy to climb up there; we just never did it before because it involves going through Aunt Bess's bedroom window.

The roof is cold as hell in the nighttime, but in the day there's a great view of the island and the sea beyond it. I can see over the trees that cluster around Cuddledown to New Clairmont and its garden. I can even see into the house, which has floor-to-ceiling windows in many of the ground-floor rooms. You can see a bit of Red Gate, too, and the other direction, across to Windemere, then out to the bay.

That first afternoon we spread out food on an old picnic blanket. We eat Portuguese sweet bread and runny cheeses in small wooden boxes. Berries in green cardboard. Cold bottles of fizzy lemonade.

We resolve to come here every day. All summer. This roof is the best place in the world.

"If I die," I say as we look at the view, "I mean, when I die, throw my ashes in the water of the tiny beach. Then when you miss me, you can climb up here, look down, and think how awesome I was."

"Or we could go down and swim in you," says Johnny. "If we missed you really badly."

"Ew."

"You're the one who wanted to be in the water of the tiny beach."

"I just meant, I love it here. It'd be a grand place to have my ashes."

"Yeah," says Johnny. "It would be."

Mirren and Gat have been silent, eating chocolate-covered hazelnuts out of a blue ceramic bowl. "This is a bad conversation," Mirren says.

"It's okay," says Johnny.

"I don't want my ashes here," says Gat.

"Why not?" I say. "We could all be together in the tiny beach."

"And the littles will swim in us!" yells Johnny.

"You're grossing me out," snaps Mirren.

"It's not actually that different from all the times I've peed in there," says Johnny.

"Gack."

"Oh, come on, everyone pees in there."

"I don't," says Mirren.

"Yes, you do," he says. "If the tiny beach water isn't made of pee now, after all these years of us peeing in it, a few ashes aren't going to ruin it."

"Do you guys ever plan out your funeral?" I ask.

"What do you mean?" Johnny crinkles his nose.

"You know, in Tom Sawyer, when everyone thinks Tom and Huck and what's-his-name?"

"Joe Harper," says Gat.

"Yeah, they think Tom, Huck, and Joe Harper are dead. The boys go to their own funeral and hear all the nice memories the townspeople have of them. After I read that, I always thought about my own funeral. Like, what kind of flowers and where I'd want my ashes. And the eulogy, too, saying how I was transcendentally awesome and won the Nobel Prize and the Olympics."

"What did you win the Olympics for?" asks Gat.

"Maybe handball."

"Is there handball in the Olympics?"

"Yes."

"Do you even play handball?"

"Not yet."

"You better get started."

"Most people plan their weddings," says Mirren. "I used to plan my wedding."

"Guys don't plan their weddings," says Johnny.

"If I married Drake I'd have all yellow flowers," Mirren

says. "Yellow flowers everywhere. And a spring yellow dress, like a normal wedding dress only yellow. And he would wear a yellow cummerbund."

"He would have to love you very, very much to wear a yellow cummerbund," I tell her.

"Yeah," says Mirren. "But Drake would do it."

"I'll tell you what I don't want at my funeral," says Johnny. "I don't want a bunch of New York art-world types who don't even know me standing around in a stupid-ass reception room."

"I don't want religious people talking about a God I don't believe in," says Gat.

"Or a bunch of fake girls acting all sad and then putting lip gloss on in the bathroom and fixing their hair," says Mirren.

"God," I quip, "you make it sound like funerals aren't any fun."

"Seriously, Cady," says Mirren. "You should plan your wedding, not your funeral. Don't be morbid."

"What if I never get married? What if I don't want to get married?"

"Plan your book party, then. Or your art opening."

"She's winning the Olympics and the Nobel Prize," says Gat. "She can plan parties for those."

"Okay, fine," I say. "Let's plan my Olympic handball party. If it'll make you happy."

So we do. Chocolate handballs wrapped in blue fondant. A gold dress for me. Champagne flutes with tiny gold balls inside. We discuss whether people wear weird goggles for handball like they do for racquetball and decide that for purposes of our party, they do. All the guests will wear gold handball goggles for the duration.

"Do you play on a handball *team*?" asks Gat. "I mean, will

there be a whole crew of Amazonian handball goddesses there, celebrating victory with you? Or did you win it by your lonesome?"

"I have no idea."

"You really have to start educating yourself about this," says Gat. "Or you're never going to win the gold. We'll have to rethink the whole party if you only get the silver."

LIFE FEELS BEAUTIFUL that day.

The four of us Liars, we have always been.

We always will be.

No matter what happens as we go to college, grow old, build lives for ourselves; no matter if Gat and I are together or not. No matter where we go, we will always be able to line up on the roof of Cuddledown and gaze at the sea.

This island is ours. Here, in some way, we are young forever.

46

DAYS THAT FOLLOW are darker. Rarely do the Liars want to go anywhere. Mirren has a sore throat and body aches. She stays mainly in Cuddledown. She paints pictures to hang in the hallways and makes rows of shells along the edges of the countertops. Dishes pile in the sink and on the coffee table. DVDs and books are in messy stacks all over the great room. The beds lie unmade and the bathrooms have a damp, mildewy smell.

Johnny eats cheese with his fingers and watches British TV comedies. One day he collects a row of old tea bags, soggy ones, and tosses them into a mug filled with orange juice.

"What are you doing?" I ask.

"Biggest splash gets the most points."

"But why?"

"My mind works in mysterious ways," says Johnny. "I find underhand is generally the best technique."

I help him figure out a point system. Five points for a sprinkle, ten for a puddle, twenty for a decorative pattern on the wall behind the mug.

We go through a whole bottle of fresh-squeezed juice. When he's done, Johnny leaves the mug and the mangled, leaking tea bags where they lie.

I don't clean up, either.

Gat has a list of the hundred greatest novels ever written, and he's pushing his way through whatever he's been able to find on the island. He marks them with sticky notes and reads passages aloud. *Invisible Man. A Passage to India. The Magnificent Ambersons.* I only half pay attention when he reads, because Gat has not kissed me or reached out to me since we agreed to act normal.

I think he avoids being alone with me.

I avoid being alone with him, too, because my whole body sings to be near him, because every movement he makes is charged with electricity. I often think of putting my arms around him or running my fingers along his lips. When I let my thoughts go there—if for a moment Johnny and Mirren are out of sight, if for even a second we are alone—the sharp pain of unrequited love invites the migraine in.

These days she is a gnarled crone, touching the raw flesh

of my brain with her cruel fingernails. She pokes my exposed nerves, exploring whether she'll take up residence in my skull. If she gets in, I'm confined to my bedroom for a day or maybe two.

We eat lunch on the roof most days.

I suppose they do it when I'm ill, too.

Every now and then a bottle rolls off the roof and the glass smashes. In fact, there are shards and shards of splintered glass, sticky with lemonade, all over the porch.

Flies buzz around, attracted by the sugar.

47

END OF THE second week, I find Johnny alone in the yard, building a structure out of Lego pieces he must have found at Red Gate.

I've got pickles, cheese straws, and leftover grilled tuna from the New Clairmont kitchen. We decide not to go on the roof since it's just the two of us. We open the containers and line them up on the edge of the dirty porch. Johnny talks about how he wants to build Hogwarts out of Lego. Or a Death Star. Or, wait! Even better is a Lego tuna fish to hang in New Clairmont now that none of Granddad's taxidermy is there anymore. That's it. Too bad there's not enough Lego on this stupid island for a visionary project such as his.

"Why didn't you call or email after my accident?" I ask. I hadn't planned to bring it up. The words spring out.

"Oh, Cady."

I feel stupid asking, but I want to know.

"You don't want to talk about Lego tuna fish instead?" Johnny vamps.

"I thought maybe you were annoyed with me about those emails. The ones I sent asking about Gat."

"No, no." Johnny wipes his hands on his T-shirt. "I disappeared because I'm an asshole. Because I don't think through my choices and I've seen too many action movies and I'm kind of a follower."

"Really? I don't think that about you."

"It's an undeniable fact."

"You weren't mad?"

"I was just a stupid fuck. But not mad. Never mad. I'm sorry, Cadence."

"Thanks."

He picks up a handful of Legos and starts fitting them together.

"Why did Gat disappear? Do you know?"

Johnny sighs. "That's another question."

"He told me I don't know the real him."

"Could be true."

"He doesn't want to discuss my accident. Or what happened with us that summer. He wants us to act normal and like nothing happened."

Johnny's lined his Legos up in stripes: blue, white, and green. "Gat had been shitty to that girl Raquel, by starting up with you. He knew it wasn't right and he hated himself for that."

"Okay."

"He didn't want to be that kind of guy. He wants to be a

good person. And he was really angry that summer, about all kinds of things. When he wasn't there for you, he hated himself even more."

"You think?"

"I'm guessing," says Johnny.

"Is he going out with anyone?"

"Aw, Cady," says Johnny. "He's a pretentious ass. I love him like a brother, but you're too good for him. Go find yourself a nice Vermont guy with muscles like Drake Loggerhead." Then he cracks up laughing.

"You're useless."

"I can't deny it," he answers. "But you've got to stop being such a mushball."

48

GIVEAWAY: *Charmed Life*, by Diana Wynne Jones.

It's one of the Chrestomanci stories Mummy read to me and Gat the year we were eight. I've reread it several times since then, but I doubt Gat has.

I open the book and write on the title page. *For Gat with everything, everything. Cady.*

I head to Cuddledown early the next morning, stepping over old teacups and DVDs. I knock on Gat's bedroom door.

No answer.

I knock again, then push it open.

It used to be Taft's room. It's full of bears and model boats, plus Gat-like piles of books, empty bags of potato chips, cashews crushed underfoot. Half-full bottles of juice and soda, CDs, the Scrabble box with most of its tiles spilled across the floor. It's as bad as the rest of the house, if not worse.

Anyway, he's not there. He must be at the beach.

I leave the book on his pillow.

49

THAT NIGHT, GAT and I find ourselves alone on the roof of Cuddledown. Mirren felt sick and Johnny took her downstairs for some tea.

Voices and music float from New Clairmont, where the aunts and Granddad are eating blueberry pie and drinking port. The littles are watching a movie in the living room.

Gat walks the slant of the roof, all the way down to the gutter and up again. It seems dangerous, so easy to fall—but he is fearless.

Now is when I can talk to him.

Now is when we can stop pretending to be normal.

I am looking for the right words, the best way to start.

Suddenly he climbs back to where I'm sitting in three big steps. "You are very, very beautiful, Cady," he says.

"It's the moonlight. Makes all the girls look pretty."

"I think you're beautiful always and forever." He is silhouetted against the moon. "Have you got a boyfriend in Vermont?"

Of course I don't. I have never had a boyfriend except for him. "My boyfriend is named Percocet," I say. "We're very close. I even went to Europe with him last summer."

"God." Gat is annoyed. Stands and walks back down to the edge of the roof.

"Joking."

Gat's back is to me. "You say we shouldn't feel sorry for you—"

"Yes."

"—but then you come out with these statements. *My boyfriend is named Percocet.* Or, *I stared at the base of the blue Italian toilet.* And it's clear you want *everyone* to feel sorry for you. And we would, I would, but you have no idea how lucky you are."

My face flushes.

He is right.

I do want people to feel sorry for me. I do.

And then I don't.

I do.

And then I don't.

"I'm sorry," I say.

"Harris sent you to Europe for eight weeks. You think he'll *ever* send Johnny or Mirren? No. And he wouldn't send me, no matter what. Just think before you complain about stuff other people would love to have."

I flinch. "Granddad sent me to Europe?"

"Come on," says Gat, bitter. "Did you really think your father paid for that trip?"

I know immediately that he is telling the truth.

Of course Dad didn't pay for the trip. There's no way he could have. College professors don't fly first-class and stay in five-star hotels.

128

So used to summers on Beechwood, to endlessly st
pantries and multiple motorboats and a staff quietly gi
steaks and washing linens—I didn't even think about v
that money might be coming from.

Granddad sent me to Europe. Why?

Why wouldn't Mummy go with me, if the trip was a gift
from Granddad? And why would Dad even take that money
from my grandfather?

"You have a life stretching out in front of you with a million
possibilities," Gat says. "It—it grates on me when you ask for
sympathy, that's all."

Gat, my Gat.

He is right. He is.

But he also doesn't understand.

"I know no one's beating me," I say, feeling defensive all of
a sudden. "I know I have plenty of money and a good education. Food on the table. I'm not dying of cancer. Lots of people
have it much worse than I. And I do know I was lucky to go to
Europe. I shouldn't complain about it or be ungrateful."

"Okay, then."

"But listen. You have no idea what it feels like to have headaches like this. No idea. It hurts," I say—and I realize tears are
running down my face, though I'm not sobbing. "It makes it
hard to be alive, some days. A lot of times I wish I were dead,
I truly do, just to make the pain stop."

"You do not," he says harshly. "You do not wish you were
dead. Don't say that."

"I just want the pain to be over," I say. "On the days the pills
don't work. I want it to end and I would do anything—really,
anything—if I knew for sure it would end the pain."

There is a silence. He walks down to the bottom edge of

the roof, facing away from me. "What do you do then? When it's like that?"

"Nothing. I lie there and wait, and remind myself over and over that it doesn't last forever. That there will be another day and after that, yet another day. One of those days, I'll get up and eat breakfast and feel okay."

"Another day."

"Yes."

Now he turns and bounds up the roof in a couple steps. Suddenly his arms are around me, and we are clinging to each other.

He is shivering slightly and he kisses my neck with cold lips. We stay like that, enfolded in each other's arms, for a minute or two,

and it feels like the universe is reorganizing itself,

and I know any anger we felt has disappeared.

Gat kisses me on the lips, and touches my cheek.

I love him.

I have always loved him.

We stay up there on the roof for a very, very long time. Forever.

50

MIRREN HAS BEEN getting ill more and more often. She gets up late, paints her nails, lies in the sun, and stares at pictures of African landscapes in a big coffee-table book. But she won't snorkel. Won't sail. Won't play tennis or go to Edgartown.

I bring her jelly beans from New Clairmont. Mirren loves jelly beans.

Today, she and I lie out on the tiny beach. We read magazines I stole from the twins and eat baby carrots. Mirren has headphones on. She keeps listening to the same song over and over on my iPhone.

> Our youth is wasted
> We will not waste it
> Remember my name
> 'Cause we made history
> Na na na na, na na na

I POKE MIRREN with a carrot.

"What?"

"You have to stop singing or I can't be responsible for my actions."

Mirren turns to me, serious. Pulls out the ear buds. "Can I tell you something, Cady?"

"Sure."

"About you and Gat. I heard you two come downstairs last night."

"So?"

"I think you should leave him alone."

"What?"

"It's going to end badly and mess everything up."

"I love him," I say. "You know I've always loved him."

"You're making things hard for him. Harder than they already are. You're going to hurt him."

"That's not true. He'll probably hurt me."

"Well, that could happen, too. It's not a good idea for you guys to be together."

"Don't you see I would rather be hurt by Gat than be closed off from him?" I say, sitting up. "I'd a million times rather live and risk and have it all end badly than stay in the box I've been in for the past two years. It's a tiny box, Mirren. Me and Mummy. Me and my pills. Me and my pain. I don't want to live there anymore."

A silence hangs in the air.

"I've never had a boyfriend," Mirren blurts.

I look into her eyes. There are tears. "What about Drake Loggerhead? What about the yellow roses and the sexual intercourse?" I ask.

She looks down. "I lied."

"Why?"

"You know how, when you come to Beechwood, it's a different world? You don't have to be who you are back home. You can be somebody better, maybe."

I nod.

"That first day you came back I noticed Gat. He looked at you like you were the brightest planet in the galaxy."

"He did?"

"I want someone to look at me that way so much, Cady. So much. And I didn't mean to, but I found myself lying. I'm sorry."

I don't know what to say. I take a deep breath.

Mirren snaps. "Don't gasp. Okay? It's fine. It's fine if I never have a boyfriend at all. It's fine if not one person ever loves me, all right? It's perfectly tolerable."

Mummy's voice calls from somewhere by New Clairmont. "Cadence! Can you hear me?"

132

I yell back. "What do you want?"

"The cook is off today. I'm starting lunch. Come slice to-matoes."

"In a minute." I sigh and look at Mirren. "I have to go."

She doesn't answer. I pull my hoodie on and trudge up the path to New Clairmont.

In the kitchen, Mummy hands me a special tomato knife and starts to talk.

Natter natter, you're always on the tiny beach.

Natter natter, you should play with the littles.

Granddad won't be here forever.

Do you know you have a sunburn?

I slice and slice, a basketful of strangely shaped heirloom tomatoes. They are yellow, green, and smoky red.

51

MY THIRD WEEK on-island is ticking by and a migraine takes me out for two days. Or maybe three. I can't even tell. The pills in my bottle are getting low, though I filled my prescription before we left home.

I wonder if Mummy is taking them. Maybe she has always been taking them.

Or maybe the twins have been coming in my room again, lifting things they don't need. Maybe they're users.

Or maybe I am taking more than I know. Popping extra in a haze of pain. Forgetting my last dose.

I am scared to tell Mummy I need more.

When I feel stable I come to Cuddledown again. The sun hovers low in the sky. The porch is covered with broken bottles. Inside, the ribbons have fallen from the ceiling and lie twisted on the floor. The dishes in the sink are dry and encrusted. The quilts that cover the dining table are dirty. The coffee table is stained with circular marks from mugs of tea.

I find the Liars clustered in Mirren's bedroom, all looking at the Bible.

"Scrabble word argument," says Mirren as soon as I enter. She closes the book. "Gat was right, as usual. You're always eff-ing right, Gat. Girls don't like that in a guy, you know."

The Scrabble tiles are scattered across the great room floor. I saw them when I walked in.

They haven't been playing.

"What did you guys do the past few days?" I ask.

"Oh, God," says Johnny, stretching out on Mirren's bed. "I forget already."

"It was Fourth of July," says Mirren. "We went to supper at New Clairmont and then everyone went out in the big motor-boat to see the Vineyard fireworks."

"Today we went to the Nantucket doughnut shop," says Gat.

They never go anywhere. Ever. Never see anyone. Now while I've been sick, they went everywhere, saw everyone?

"Downyflake," I say. "That's the name of the doughnut shop."

"Yeah. They were the most amazing doughnuts," says Johnny.

"You hate cake doughnuts."

"Of course," says Mirren. "But we didn't get the cake, we got glazed twists."

"And Boston cream," says Gat.

"And jelly," says Johnny.

But I know Downyflake only makes cake doughnuts. No glazed. No Boston cream. No jelly.

Why are they lying?

52

I EAT SUPPER with Mummy and the littles at New Clairmont, but that night I am hit with a migraine again. It's worse than the one before. I lie in my darkened room. Scavenger birds peck at the oozing matter that leaks from my crushed skull.

I open my eyes and Gat stands over me. I see him through a haze. Light shines through the curtains, so it must be day.

Gat never comes to Windemere. But here he is. Looking at the graph paper on my wall. At the sticky notes. At the new memories and information I've added since I've been here, notes about Gran's dogs dying, Granddad and the ivory goose, Gat giving me the Moriarty book, the aunts fighting about the Boston house.

"Don't read my papers," I moan. "Don't."

He steps back. "It's up there for anyone to see. Sorry."

I turn on my side to press my cheek against the hot pillow.

"I didn't know you were collecting stories." Gat sits on the bed. Reaches out and takes my hand.

"I'm trying to remember what happened that nobody wants to talk about," I say. "Including you."

"I want to talk about it."

"You do?"

He is staring at the floor. "I had a girlfriend, two summers ago."

"I know. I knew all along."

"But I never told you."

"No, you didn't."

"I fell for you so hard, Cady. There was no stopping it. I know I should have told you everything and I should have broken it off with Raquel right away. It was just—she was back home, and I never see you all year, and my phone didn't work here, and I kept getting packages from her. And letters. All summer."

I look at him.

"I was a coward," Gat says.

"Yeah."

"It was cruel. To you and to her, too."

My face burns with remembered jealousy.

"I am sorry, Cady," Gat goes on. "That's what I should have said to you the first day we got here this year. I was wrong and I'm sorry."

I nod. It is nice to hear him say that. I wish I weren't so high.

"Half the time I hate myself for all the things I've done," says Gat. "But the thing that makes me really messed up is the contradiction: when I'm not hating myself, I feel righteous and victimized. Like the world is so unfair."

"Why do you hate yourself?"

And before I know it, Gat is lying on the bed next to me. His cold fingers wrap around my hot ones, and his face is close to mine. He kisses me. "Because I want things I can't have," he whispers.

But he has me. Doesn't he know he already has me?

Or is Gat talking about something else, something else he can't have? Some material thing, some dream of something?

I am sweaty and my head hurts and I can't think clearly. "Mirren says it'll end badly and I should leave you alone," I tell him.

He kisses me again.

"Someone did something to me that is too awful to remember," I whisper.

"I love you," he says.

We hold each other and kiss for a long time.

The pain in my head fades, a little. But not all the way.

I OPEN MY eyes and the clock reads midnight.

Gat is gone.

I pull the shades and look out the window, lifting the sash to get some air.

Aunt Carrie is walking in her nightgown again. Passing by Windemere, scratching her too-thin arms in the moonlight. She doesn't even have her shearling boots on this time.

Over at Red Gate I can hear Will crying from a nightmare. "Mommy! Mommy, I need you!"

But Carrie either doesn't hear him, or else she will not go. She veers away and heads up the path toward New Clairmont.

53

GIVEAWAY: A PLASTIC box of Legos.

I've given away all my books now. I gave a few to the littles, one to Gat, and went with Aunt Bess to donate the rest to a charity shop on the Vineyard.

This morning I rummage through the attic. There's a box of Legos there, so I bring them to Johnny. I find him alone in the Cuddledown great room, hurling bits of Play-Doh at the wall and watching the colors stain the white paint.

He sees the Legos and shakes his head.

"For your tuna fish," I explain. "Now you'll have enough."

"I'm not gonna build it," he says.

"Why not?"

"Too much work," he says. "Give them to Will."

"Don't you have Will's Legos down here?"

"I brought them back. Little guy was starved for them," Johnny says. "He'll be happy to have more."

I bring them to Will at lunch. There are little Lego people and lots of parts for building cars.

He is ridiculously happy. He and Taft build cars all through the meal. They don't even eat.

54

THAT SAME AFTERNOON, the Liars get the kayaks out. "What are you doing?" I ask.

"Going round the point to this place we know," says Johnny. "We've done it before."

"Cady shouldn't come," says Mirren.

"Why not?" asks Johnny.

"Because of her head!" shouts Mirren. "What if she hurts her head again, and her migraines get even worse? God, do you even have a brain, Johnny?"

"Why are you yelling?" yells Johnny. "Don't be so bossy."

Why don't they want me to come?

"You can come, Cadence," says Gat. "It's fine if she comes."

I don't want to tag along when I'm not wanted—but Gat pats the kayak seat in front of him and I climb in.

I do not really want to be separate from them.

Ever.

We paddle the two-person kayaks around the bay side under Windemere to an inlet. Mummy's house sits on an overhang. Beneath it is a cluster of craggy rocks that almost feels like a cave. We pull the kayaks onto the rocks and climb to where it's dry and cool.

Mirren is seasick, though we were only in the kayaks for a few minutes. She is sick so often now, it's no surprise. She lies down with her arms over her face. I half expect the boys to unpack a picnic—they have a canvas bag with them—but instead Gat and Johnny begin climbing the rocks. They've done it before, I can tell. They're barefoot, and they climb to a high point twenty-five feet above the water, stopping on a ledge that hangs over the sea.

I watch them until they are settled. "What are you doing?"

"We are being very, very manly," Johnny calls back. His voice echoes.

Gat laughs.

"No, really," I say.

"You might think we are city boys, but truth is, we are full of masculinity and testosterone."

"Are not."

"Are too."

"Oh, please. I'm coming up with you."

"No, don't!" says Mirren.

"Johnny baited me," I say. "Now I have to." I begin climbing in the same direction the boys went. The rocks are cold under my hands, slicker than I expected.

"Don't," Mirren repeats. "This is why I didn't want you to come."

"Why did you come, then?" I ask. "Are you going up there?"

"I jumped last time," Mirren admits. "Once was enough."

"They're jumping?" It doesn't even look possible.

"Stop, Cady. It's dangerous," says Gat.

And before I can climb farther, Johnny holds his nose and jumps. He plummets feetfirst from the high rock.

I scream.

He hits the water with force and the sea is filled with rocks here. There's no telling how deep or shallow it is. He could seriously die doing this. He could—but he pops up, shaking the water off his short yellow hair and whooping.

"You're crazy!" I scold.

Then Gat jumps. Whereas Johnny kicked and hollered as he went down, Gat is silent, legs together. He slices into the icy water with hardly a splash. He comes up happy, squeezing water out of his T-shirt as he climbs back onto the dry rocks.

"They're idiots," says Mirren.

I look up at the rocks from which they jumped. It seems impossible anyone could survive.

And suddenly, I want to do it. I start climbing again.

"Don't, Cady," says Gat. "Please don't."

"You just did," I say. "And you said it was fine if I came."

Mirren sits up, her face pale. "I want to go home now," she says urgently. "I don't feel well."

"Please don't, Cady, it's rocky," calls Johnny. "We shouldn't have brought you."

"I'm not an invalid," I say. "I know how to swim."

"That's not it, it's—it's not a good idea."

"Why is it a good idea for you and not a good idea for me?" I snap. I am nearly at the top. My fingertips are already beginning to blister with clutching the rock. Adrenaline shoots through my bloodstream.

"We were being stupid," says Gat.

"Showing off," says Johnny.

"Come down, please." Mirren is crying now.

I do not come down. I am sitting, knees to my chest, on the ledge from which the boys jumped. I look at the sea churning beneath me. Dark shapes lurk beneath the surface of the water, but I can also see an open space. If I position my jump right, I will hit deep water.

"Always do what you are afraid to do!" I call out.

141

"That's a stupid-ass motto," says Mirren. "I told you that before."

I will prove myself strong, when they think I am sick.

I will prove myself brave, when they think I am weak.

It's windy on this high rock. Mirren is sobbing. Gat and Johnny are shouting at me.

I close my eyes and jump.

The shock of the water is electric. Thrilling. My leg scrapes a rock, my left leg. I plunge down,

down to rocky rocky bottom, and

I can see the base of Beechwood Island and

my arms and legs feel numb but my fingers are cold. Slices of seaweed go past as I fall.

And then I am up again, and breathing.

I'm okay,

my head is okay,

no one needs to cry for me or worry about me.

I am fine,

I am alive.

I swim to shore.

SOMETIMES I WONDER if reality splits. In *Charmed Life*, that book I gave Gat, there are parallel universes in which different events have happened to the same people. An alternate choice has been made, or an accident has turned out differently. Everyone has duplicates of themselves in these other worlds. Different selves with different lives, different luck.

Variations.

I wonder, for example, if there's a variation of today where I die going off that cliff. I have a funeral where my ashes are scattered at the tiny beach. A million flowering peonies surround my drowned body as people sob in penance and misery. I am a beautiful corpse.

I wonder if there's another variation in which Johnny is hurt, his legs and back crushed against the rocks. We can't call emergency services and we have to paddle back in the kayak with his nerves severed. By the time we helicopter him to the hospital on the mainland, he's never going to walk again.

Or another variation, in which I don't go with the Liars in the kayaks at all. I let them push me away. They keep going places without me and telling me small lies. We grow apart, bit by bit, and eventually our summer idyll is ruined forever.

It seems to me more than likely that these variations exist.

55

THAT NIGHT I wake, cold. I've kicked my blankets off and the window is open. I sit up too fast and my head spins.

A memory.

Aunt Carrie, crying. Bent over with snot running down her face, not even bothering to wipe it off. She's doubled over, she's shaking, she might throw up. It's dark out, and she's wearing a white cotton blouse with a wind jacket over it—Johnny's blue-checked one.

Why is she wearing Johnny's wind jacket?

Why is she so sad?

I get up and find a sweatshirt and shoes. I grab a flashlight and head to Cuddledown. The great room is empty and lit by moonlight. Bottles litter the kitchen counter. Someone left a sliced apple out and it's browning. I can smell it.

Mirren is here. I didn't see her before. She's tucked beneath a striped afghan, leaning against the couch.

"You're up," she whispers.

"I came looking for you."

"How come?"

"I had this memory. Aunt Carrie was crying. She was wearing Johnny's coat. Do you remember Carrie crying?"

"Sometimes."

"But summer fifteen, when she had that short haircut?"

"No," says Mirren.

"How come you're not asleep?" I ask.

Mirren shakes her head. "I don't know."

I sit down. "Can I ask you a question?"

"Sure."

"I need you to tell me what happened before my accident. And after. You always say nothing important—but something must have happened to me besides hitting my head during a nighttime swim."

"Uh-huh."

"Do you know what it was?"

"Penny said the doctors want it left alone. You'll remember in your own time and no one should push it on you."

"But I am asking, Mirren. I need to know."

She puts her head down on her knees. Thinking. "What is your best guess?" she finally says.

"I—I suppose I was the victim of something." It is hard to say these words. "I suppose that I was raped or attacked or some godforsaken something. That's the kind of thing that makes people have amnesia, isn't it?"

Mirren rubs her lips. "I don't know what to tell you," she says.

"Tell me what happened," I say.

"It was a messed-up summer."

"How so?"

"That's all I can say, my darling Cady."

"Why won't you ever leave Cuddledown?" I ask suddenly. "You hardly ever leave except to go to the tiny beach."

"I went kayaking today," she says.

"But you got sick. Do you have that fear?" I ask. "That fear of going out? Agoraphobia?"

"I don't feel well, Cady," says Mirren, defensive. "I am cold all the time, I can't stop shivering. My throat is raw. If you felt this way, you wouldn't go out, either."

I feel worse than that all the time, but for once I don't mention my headaches. "We should tell Bess, then. Take you to the doctor."

Mirren shakes her head. "It's just a stupid cold I can't shake. I'm being a baby about it. Will you get me a ginger ale?"

I cannot argue anymore. I get her a ginger ale and we turn on the television.

56

IN THE MORNING, there is a tire swing hanging from the tree on the lawn of Windemere. The same way one used to hang from the huge old maple in front of Clairmont.

It is perfect.

Just like the one Granny Tipper spun me on.

Dad.

Granddad.

Mummy.

Like the one Gat and I kissed on in the middle of the night.

I remember now, summer fifteen, Johnny, Mirren, Gat, and I squashed into that Clairmont swing together. We were much too big to fit. We elbowed each other and rearranged ourselves. We giggled and complained. Accused each other of having big asses. Accused each other of being smelly and rearranged again.

Finally we got settled. Then we couldn't spin. We were jammed so hard into the swing, there was no way to get moving. We yelled and yelled for a push. The twins walked by and refused to help. Finally, Taft and Will came out of Clairmont and did our bidding. Grunting, they pushed us in a wide circle. Our weight was such that after they let us go, we spun faster and faster, laughing so hard we felt dizzy and sick.

All four of us Liars. I remember that now.

THIS NEW SWING looks strong. The knots are tied carefully.

Inside the tire is an envelope.

Gat's handwriting: *For Cady.*

I open the envelope.

More than a dozen dried beach roses spill out.

57

ONCE UPON A time there was a king who had three beautiful daughters. He gave them whatever their hearts desired, and when they grew of age their marriages were celebrated with grand festivities. When the youngest daughter gave birth to a baby girl, the king and queen were overjoyed. Soon afterward, the middle daughter gave birth to a girl of her own, and the celebrations were repeated.

Last, the eldest daughter gave birth to twin boys—but alas, all was not as one might hope. One of the twins was human, a bouncing baby boy; the other was no more than a mouseling.

There was no celebration. No announcements were made.

The eldest daughter was consumed with shame. One of her children was nothing but an animal. He would never sparkle, sunburnt and blessed, the way members of the royal family were expected to do.

The children grew, and the mouseling as well. He was clever and always kept his whiskers clean. He was smarter and more curious than his brother or his cousins.

Still, he disgusted the king and he disgusted the queen. As soon as she was able, his mother set the mouseling on his feet, gave him a small satchel in which she had placed a blueberry and some nuts, and sent him off to see the world.

Set out he did, for the mouseling had seen enough of courtly life to know that should he stay home he would always be a *dirty secret, a source of humiliation to his mother and anyone who knew of him.*

He did not even look back at the castle that had been his home.

There, he would never even have a name.

Now, he was free to go forth and make a name for himself in the wide, wide world.

And maybe,
just maybe,
he'd come back one day,
and burn that
fucking
palace
to the ground.

PART FOUR

Look, a Fire

58

LOOK.

A fire.

There on the southern tip of Beechwood Island. Where the maple tree stands over the wide lawn.

The house is alight. The flames shoot high, brightening the sky.

There is no one here to help.

Far in the distance, I can see the Vineyard firefighters, making their way across the bay in a lighted boat.

Even farther away, the Woods Hole fire boat chugs toward the fire that we set.

Gat, Johnny, Mirren, and me.

We set this fire and it is burning down Clairmont.

Burning down the palace, the palace of the king who had three beautiful daughters.

We set it.

Me, Johnny, Gat, and Mirren.

I remember this now,

in a rush that hits me so hard I fall,

and I plunge down,

down to rocky rocky bottom, and

I can see the base of Beechwood Island and

my arms and legs feel numb but my fingers are cold. Slices of seaweed go past as I fall.

And then I am up again, and breathing,

And Clairmont is burning.

I AM IN my bed in Windemere, in the early light of dawn.

It is the first day of my last week on the island. I stumble to the window, wrapped in my blanket.

There is New Clairmont. All hard modernity and Japanese garden.

I see it for what it is, now. It is a house built on ashes. Ashes of the life Granddad shared with Gran, ashes of the maple from which the tire swing flew, ashes of the old Victorian house with the porch and the hammock. The new house is built on the grave of all the trophies and symbols of the family: the New Yorker cartoons, the taxidermy, the embroidered pillows, the family portraits.

We burned them all.

On a night when Granddad and the rest had taken boats across the bay,

when the staff was off duty

and we Liars were alone on the island,

the four of us did what we were afraid to do.

We burned not a home, but a symbol.

We burned a symbol to the ground.

59

THE CUDDLEDOWN DOOR is locked. I bang until Johnny appears, wearing the clothes he had on last night. "I'm making pretentious tea," he says.

"Did you sleep in your clothes?"

"Yes."

"We set a fire," I tell him, still standing in the doorway.

They will not lie to me anymore. Go places without me, make decisions without me.

I understand our story now. We are criminals. A band of four.

Johnny looks me in the eyes for a long time but doesn't say a word. Eventually he turns and goes into the kitchen. I follow. Johnny pours hot water from the kettle into teacups.

"What else do you remember?" he asks.

I hesitate.

I can see the fire. The smoke. How huge Clairmont looked as it burned.

I know, irrevocably and certainly, that we set it.

I can see Mirren's hand, her chipped gold nail polish, holding a jug of gas for the motorboats.

Johnny's feet, running down the stairs from Clairmont to the boathouse.

Granddad, holding on to a tree, his face lit by the glow of a bonfire.

No. Correction.

The glow of his house, burning to the ground.

But these are memories I've had all along. I just know where to fit them now.

"Not everything," I tell Johnny. "I just know we set the fire. I can see the flames."

He lies down on the floor of the kitchen and stretches his arms over his head.

"Are you okay?" I ask.

"I'm fucking tired. If you want to know." Johnny rolls over

on his face and pushes his nose against the tile. "They said they weren't speaking anymore," he mumbles into the floor. "They said it was over and they were cutting off from each other."

"Who?"

"The aunties."

I lie down on the floor next to him so I can hear what he's saying.

"The aunties got drunk, night after night," Johnny mumbles, as if it's hard to choke the words out. "And angrier, every time. Screaming at each other. Staggering around the lawn. Granddad did nothing but fuel them. We watched them quarrel over Gran's things and the art that hung in Clairmont—but real estate and money most of all. Granddad was drunk on his own power and my mother wanted me to make a play for the money. Because I was the oldest boy. She pushed me and pushed me—I don't know. To be the bright young heir. To talk badly of you as the eldest. To be the educated white hope of the future of democracy, some bullshit. She'd lost Granddad's favor, and she wanted me to get it so she didn't lose her inheritance."

As he talks, memories flash across my skull, so hard and bright they hurt. I flinch and put my hands over my eyes.

"Do you remember any more about the fire?" he asks gently. "Is it coming back?"

I close my eyes for a moment and try. "No, not that. But other things."

Johnny reaches out and takes my hand.

60

SPRING BEFORE SUMMER fifteen, Mummy made me write to Granddad. Nothing blatant. "Thinking of you and your loss today. Hoping you are well."

I sent actual cards—heavy cream stock with *Cadence Sinclair Eastman* printed across the top. *Dear Granddad, I just rode in a 5K bike ride for cancer research. Tennis team starts up next week. Our book club is reading* Brideshead Revisited. *Love you.*

"Just remind him that you care," said Mummy. "And that you're a good person. Well-rounded and a credit to the family."

I complained. Writing the letters seemed false. Of course I cared. I loved Granddad and I did think about him. But I didn't want to write these reminders of my excellence every two weeks.

"He's very impressionable right now," said Mummy. "He's suffering. Thinking about the future. You're the first grandchild."

"Johnny's only three weeks younger."

"That's my point. Johnny's a boy and he's only three weeks younger. So write the letter."

I did as she asked.

ON BEECHWOOD SUMMER fifteen, the aunties filled in for Gran, making slumps and fussing around Granddad as if he hadn't been living alone in Boston since Tipper died in October. But they were quarrelsome. They no longer had the glue of Gran keeping them together, and they fought over their memories, her jewelry, the clothes in her closet, her shoes, even. These affairs had not been settled in October. People's feelings had been too delicate then. It had all been left for the summer. When we got to Beechwood in late June, Bess had already inventoried Gran's Boston possessions and now began with those in Clairmont. The aunts had copies on their tablets and pulled them up regularly.

"I always loved that jade tree ornament."

"I'm surprised you remember it. You never helped decorate."

"Who do you think took the tree down? Every year I wrapped all the ornaments in tissue paper."

"Martyr."

"Here are the pearl earrings Mother promised me."

"The black pearls? She said I could have them."

The aunts began to blur into one another as the days of the summer ticked past. Argument after argument, old injuries were rehashed and threaded through new ones.

Variations.

"Tell Granddad how much you love the embroidered tablecloths," Mummy told me.

"I don't love them."

"He won't say no to you." The two of us were alone in the Windemere kitchen. She was drunk. "You love me, don't you, Cadence? You're all I have now. You're not like Dad."

"I just don't care about tablecloths."

"So lie. Tell him the ones from the Boston house. The cream ones with the embroidery."

It was easiest to tell her I would.

And later, I told her I had.

But Bess had asked Mirren to do the same thing,
and neither one of us
begged Granddad
for the fucking tablecloths.

61

GAT AND I went night swimming. We lay on the wooden walkway and looked at the stars. We kissed in the attic.

We fell in love.

He gave me a book. *With everything, everything.*

We didn't talk about Raquel. I couldn't ask. He didn't say.

The twins have their birthday July fourteenth, and there's always a big meal. All twelve of us were sitting at the long table on the lawn outside Clairmont. Lobsters and potatoes with caviar. Small pots of melted butter. Baby vegetables and basil. Two cakes, one vanilla and one chocolate, waited inside on the kitchen counter.

The littles were getting noisy with their lobsters, poking each other with claws and slurping meat out of the legs. Johnny told stories. Mirren and I laughed. We were surprised when Granddad walked over and wedged himself between Gat and me. "I want to ask your advice on something," he said. "The advice of youth."

"We are worldly and awesome youth," said Johnny, "so you've come to the right end of the table."

"You know," said Granddad, "I'm not getting any younger, despite my good looks."

"Yeah, yeah," I said.

"Thatcher and I are sorting through my affairs. I'm considering leaving a good portion of my estate to my alma mater."

"To Harvard? For what, Dad?" asked Mummy, who had walked over to stand behind Mirren.

Granddad smiled. "Probably to fund a student center. They'd put my name on it, out front." He nudged Gat. "What should they call it, young man, eh? What do you think?"

"Harris Sinclair Hall?" Gat ventured.

"Pah." Granddad shook his head. "We can do better. Johnny?"

"The Sinclair Center for Socialization," Johnny said, shoving zucchini into his mouth.

"And snacks," put in Mirren. "The Sinclair Center for Socialization and Snacks."

Granddad banged his hand on the table. "I like the ring of it. Not educational, but appreciated by everyone. I'm convinced. I'll call Thatcher tomorrow. My name will be on every student's favorite building."

"You'll have to die before they build it," I said.

"True. But won't you be proud to see my name up there when you're a student?"

"You're not dying before we go to college," said Mirren. "We won't allow it."

"Oh, if you insist." Granddad speared a bit of lobster tail off her plate and ate it.

We were caught up easily, Mirren, Johnny, and I—feeling the power he conferred in picturing us at Harvard, the specialness of asking our opinions and laughing at our jokes. That was how Granddad had always treated us.

"You're not being funny, Dad," Mummy snapped. "Drawing the children into it."

"We're not children," I told her. "We understand the conversation."

"No, you don't," she said, "or you wouldn't be humoring him that way."

A chill went around the table. Even the littles quieted.

Carrie lived with Ed. The two of them bought art that might or might not be valuable later. Johnny and Will went to private school. Carrie had started a jewelry boutique with her trust and ran it for a number of years until it failed. Ed earned money, and he supported her, but Carrie didn't have an income of her own. And they weren't married. He owned their apartment and she didn't.

Bess was raising four kids on her own. She had some money from her trust, like Mummy and Carrie did, but when she got divorced Brody kept the house. She hadn't worked since she got married, and before that she'd only been an assistant in the offices of a magazine. Bess was living off the trust money and spending through it.

And Mummy. The dog breeding business doesn't pay much, and Dad wanted us to sell the Burlington house so he could take half. I knew Mummy was living off her trust.

We.

We were living off her trust.

It wouldn't last forever.

So when Granddad said he might leave his money to build Harvard a student center and asked our advice, he wasn't involving the family in his financial plans.

He was making a threat.

62

A FEW EVENINGS later. Clairmont cocktail hour. It began at six or six-thirty, depending on when people wandered up the hill to the big house. The cook was fixing supper and had set out salmon mousse with little floury crackers. I went past her and pulled a bottle of white wine from the fridge for the aunties.

The littles, having been down at the big beach all afternoon, were being forced into showers and fresh clothes by Gat, Johnny, and Mirren at Red Gate, where there was an outdoor shower. Mummy, Bess, and Carrie sat around the Clairmont coffee table.

I brought wineglasses for the aunts as Granddad entered. "So, Penny," he said, pouring himself bourbon from the decanter on the sideboard, "how are you and Cady doing at Windemere this year, with the change of circumstances? Bess is worried you're lonely."

"I didn't say that," said Bess.

Carrie narrowed her eyes.

"Yes, you did," Granddad said to Bess. He motioned for me to sit down. "You talked about the five bedrooms. The renovated kitchen, and how Penny's alone now and won't need it."

"Did you, Bess?" Mummy drew breath.

Bess didn't reply. She bit her lip and looked out at the view.

"We're not lonely," Mummy told Granddad. "We adore Windemere, don't we, Cady?"

Granddad beamed at me. "You okay there, Cadence?"

I knew what I was supposed to say. "I'm more than okay there, I'm fantastic. I love Windemere because you built it specially for Mummy. I want to raise my own children there and my children's children. You are so excellent, Granddad. You are the patriarch and I revere you. I am so glad I am a Sinclair. This is the best family in America."

Not in those words. But I was meant to help Mummy keep the house by telling my grandfather that he was the big man, that he was the cause of all our happiness, and by reminding him that I was the future of the family. The all-American Sinclairs would perpetuate ourselves, tall and white and beautiful and rich, if only he let Mummy and me stay in Windemere.

I was supposed to make Granddad feel in control when his world was spinning because Gran had died. I was to beg him by praising him—never acknowledging the aggression behind his question.

My mother and her sisters were dependent on Granddad and his money. They had the best educations, a thousand chances, a thousand connections, and still they'd ended up unable to support themselves. None of them did anything useful in the world. Nothing necessary. Nothing brave. They were still little girls, trying to get in good with Daddy. He was their bread and butter, their cream and honey, too.

"It's too big for us," I told Granddad.

No one spoke as I left the room.

63

MUMMY AND I were silent on the walk back to Windemere after supper. Once the door shut behind us, she turned on me. "Why didn't you back me with your grandfather? Do you want us to lose this house?"

"We don't need it."

"I picked the paint, the tiles. I hung the flag from the porch."

"It's five bedrooms."

"We thought we'd have a bigger family." Mummy's face got tight. "But it didn't work out that way. That doesn't mean I don't deserve the house."

"Mirren and those guys could use the room."

"This is my house. You can't expect me to give it up because Bess had too many children and left her husband. You can't think it's okay for her to snatch it from me. This is our place, Cadence. We've got to look out for ourselves."

"Can you hear yourself?" I snapped. "You have a trust fund!"

"What does that have to do with it?"

"Some people have nothing. We have everything. The only person who used the family money for charity was Gran. Now she's gone and all anyone's worried about is her pearls and her ornaments and her real estate. Nobody is trying to use their money for good. Nobody is trying to make the world any better."

Mummy stood up. "You're filled with superiority, aren't you? You think you understand the world so much better than I do. I've heard Gat talking. I've seen you eating up his words like ice cream off a spoon. But you haven't paid bills, you haven't had a family, owned property, seen the world. You have no idea what you're talking about, and yet you do nothing but pass judgment."

"You are ripping up this family because you think you deserve the prettiest house."

Mummy walked to the foot of the stairs. "You go back to Clairmont tomorrow. You tell Granddad how much you love Windemere. Tell him you want to raise your own kids spending summers here. You tell him."

"No. You should stand up to him. Tell him to stop manipulating all of you. He's only acting like this because he's sad about Gran, can't you tell? Can't you help him? Or get a job so his money doesn't matter? Or give the house to Bess?"

"Listen to me, young lady." Mummy's voice was steely. "You go and talk to Granddad about Windemere or I will send you to Colorado with your father for the rest of the summer. I'll do it tomorrow. I swear, I'll take you to the airport first thing. You won't see that boyfriend of yours again. Understand?"

She had me there.

She knew about me and Gat. And she could take him away.

Would take him away.

I was in love.

I promised whatever she asked.

When I told Granddad how much I adored the house, he smiled and said he knew someday I'd have beautiful children. Then he said Bess was a grasping wench and he had no intention of giving her my house. But later, Mirren told me he'd promised Windemere to Bess.

"I'll take care of you," he'd said. "Just give me a little time to get Penny out."

64

GAT AND I went out on the tennis court in the twilight a couple nights after I fought with Mummy. We tossed balls for Fatima and Prince Philip in silence.

Finally he said, "Have you noticed Harris never calls me by my name?"

"No."

"He calls me *young man*. Like, How was your school year, young man?"

"Why?"

"It's like, if he called me *Gat* he'd be really saying, How was your school year, Indian boy whose Indian uncle lives in sin with my pure white daughter? Indian boy I caught kissing my precious Cadence?"

"You believe that's what he's thinking?"

"He can't stomach me," said Gat. "Not really. He might like me as a person, might even like Ed, but he can't say my name or look me in the eye."

It was true. Now that he said it, I could see.

"I'm not saying he wants to be the guy who only likes white people," Gat went on. "He knows he's not supposed to be that guy. He's a Democrat, he voted for Obama—but that doesn't mean he's comfortable having people of color in his beautiful family." Gat shook his head. "He's fake with us. He doesn't like the idea of Carrie with us. He doesn't call Ed *Ed*. He calls him *sir*. And he makes sure I know I'm an outsider, every chance he gets." Gat stroked Fatima's soft doggy ears. "You saw him in the attic. He wants me to stay the hell away from you."

I hadn't seen Granddad's interruption that way. I'd imagined he was embarrassed at walking in on us.

But now, suddenly, I understood what had happened.

Watch yourself, young man, Granddad had said. Your head. You could get hurt.

It was another threat.

"Did you know my uncle proposed to Carrie, back in the fall?" Gat asked.

I shook my head.

"They've been together almost nine years. He acts as a dad to Johnny and Will. He got down on his knees and proposed, Cady. He had the three of us boys there, and my mom. He'd decorated the apartment with candles and roses. We all dressed in white, and we'd brought this big meal in from this Italian place Carrie loves. He put Mozart on the stereo.

"Johnny and I were all, Ed, what's the big deal? She lives with you, dude. But the man was nervous. He'd bought a diamond ring. Anyway, she came home, and the four of us left them alone and hid in Will's room. We were supposed to all rush out with congratulations—but Carrie said no."

"I thought they didn't see a point to getting married."

"Ed sees a point. Carrie doesn't want to risk her stupid inheritance," Gat said.

"She didn't even ask Granddad?"

"That's the thing," said Gat. "Everyone's always asking Harris about everything. Why should a grown woman have to ask her father to approve her wedding?"

"Granddad wouldn't stop her."

"No," said Gat. "But back when Carrie first moved in with

Ed, Harris made it clear that all the money earmarked for her would disappear if she married him.

"The point is, Harris doesn't like Ed's color. He's a racist bastard, and so was Tipper. Yes, I like them both for a lot of reasons, and they have been more than generous letting me come here every summer. I'm willing to think that Harris doesn't even *realize* why he doesn't like my uncle, but he dislikes him enough to disinherit his eldest daughter."

Gat sighed. I loved the curve of his jaw, the hole in his T-shirt, the notes he wrote me, the way his mind worked, the way he moved his hands when he talked. I imagined, then, that I knew him completely.

I leaned in and kissed him. It still seemed so magical that I could do that, and that he would kiss me back. So magical that we showed our weaknesses to one another, our fears and our fragility. "Why didn't we ever talk about this?" I whispered.

Gat kissed me again. "I love it here," he said. "The island. Johnny and Mirren. The houses and the sound of the ocean. You."

"You too."

"Part of me doesn't want to ruin it. Doesn't want to even imagine that it isn't perfect."

I understood how he felt.

Or thought I did.

Gat and I went down to the perimeter then, and walked until we got to a wide, flat rock that looked over the harbor. The water crashed against the foot of the island. We held each other and got halfway naked and forgot, for as long as we could, every horrid detail of the beautiful Sinclair family.

65

ONCE UPON *A time there was a wealthy merchant who had three beautiful daughters. He spoiled them so much that the younger two girls did little all day but sit before the mirror, gazing at their own beauty and pinching their cheeks to make them red.*

One day the merchant had to leave on a journey. "What shall I bring you when I return?" he asked.

The youngest daughter requested gowns of silk and lace.

The middle daughter requested rubies and emeralds.

The eldest daughter requested only a rose.

The merchant was gone several months. For his youngest daughter, he filled a trunk with gowns of many colors. For his middle daughter, he scoured the markets for jewels. But only when he found himself close to home did he remember his promise of a rose for his eldest child.

He came upon a large iron fence that stretched along the road. In the distance was a dark mansion and he was pleased to see a rosebush near the fence bursting with red blooms. Several roses were easily within reach.

It was the work of a minute to cut a flower. The merchant was tucking the blossom into his saddlebag when an angry growl stopped him.

A cloaked figure stood where the merchant was certain no one had been a moment earlier. He was enormous and spoke with a deep rumble. "You take from me with no thought of payment?"

"Who are you?" the merchant asked, quaking.

"Suffice it to say I am one from whom you steal."

The merchant explained that he had promised his daughter a rose after a long journey.

"You may keep your stolen rose," said the figure, "but in exchange, give me the first of your possessions you see upon your return." He then pushed back his hood to reveal the face of a hideous beast, all teeth and snout. A wild boar combined with a jackal.

"You have crossed me," said the beast. "You will die if you cross me again."

The merchant rode home as fast as his horse would carry him. He was still a mile away when he saw his eldest daughter waiting for him on the road. "We got word you would arrive this evening!" she cried, rushing into his arms.

She was the first of his possessions he saw upon his return. He now knew what price the beast had truly asked of him.

Then what?

We all know that Beauty grows to love the beast. She grows to love him, despite what her family might think—for his charm and education, his knowledge of art and his sensitive heart.

Indeed, he is a human and always was one. He was never a wild boar/jackal at all. It was only a hideous illusion.

Trouble is, it's awfully hard to convince her father of that.

Her father sees the jaws and the snout, he hears the hideous growl, whenever Beauty brings her new husband home for a visit. It doesn't matter how civilized and erudite the husband is. It doesn't matter how kind.

The father sees a jungle animal, and his repugnance will never leave him.

66

ONE NIGHT, SUMMER fifteen, Gat tossed pebbles at my bedroom window. I put out my head to see him standing among the trees, moonlight glinting off his skin, eyes flashing.

He was waiting for me at the foot of the porch steps. "I have a dire need for chocolate," he whispered, "so I'm raiding the Clairmont pantry. You coming?"

I nodded and we walked together up the narrow path, our fingers entwined. We stepped around to the side entrance of Clairmont, the one that led to the mudroom filled with tennis racquets and beach towels. With one hand on the screen door, Gat turned and pulled me close.

His warm lips were on mine,

our hands were still together,

there, at the door to the house.

For a moment, the two of us were alone on the planet,

with all the vastness of the sky and the future and the past spreading out around us.

We tiptoed through the mudroom and into the large pantry that opened off the kitchen. The room was old-fashioned, with heavy wooden drawers and shelves for holding jams and pickles, back when the house was built. Now it stored cookies, cases of wine, potato chips, root vegetables, seltzer. We left the light off, in case someone came into the kitchen, but we were sure Granddad was the only one sleeping at Clairmont. He was never going to hear anything in the night. He wore a hearing aid by day.

We were rummaging when we heard voices. It was the aunts coming into the kitchen, their speech slurred and hysterical. "This is why people kill each other," said Bess bitterly. "I should walk out of this room before I do something I regret."

"You don't mean that," said Carrie.

"Don't tell me what I mean!" shouted Bess. "You have Ed. You don't need money like I do."

"You've already dug your claws into the Boston house," said Mummy. "Leave the island alone."

"Who did the funeral arrangements for Mother?" snapped Bess. "Who stayed by Dad's side for weeks, who went through the papers, talked to the mourners, wrote the thank-you notes?"

"You live near him," said Mummy. "You were right there."

"I was running a household with four kids and holding down a job," said Bess. "You were doing neither."

"A part-time job," said Mummy. "And if I hear you say four kids again, I'll scream."

"I was running a household, too," said Carrie.

"Either of you could have come for a week or two. You left it all to me," said Bess. "I'm the one who has to deal with Dad all year. I'm the one who runs over when he wants help. I'm the one who deals with his dementia and his grief."

"Don't say that," said Carrie. "You don't know how often he calls me. You don't know how much I have to swallow just to be a good daughter to him."

"So damn straight I want that house," continued Bess, as if she hadn't heard. "I've earned it. Who drove Mother to her doctor's appointments? Who sat by her bedside?"

"That's not fair," said Mummy. "You know I came down. Carrie came down, too."

"To visit," hissed Bess.

"You didn't have to do that stuff," said Mummy. "Nobody asked you to."

"Nobody else was there to do it. You let me do it, and never thanked me. I'm crammed into Cuddledown and it has the worst kitchen. You never even go in there, you'd be surprised how run-down it is. It's worth almost nothing. Mother fixed up the Windemere kitchen before she died, and the bathrooms at Red Gate, but Cuddledown is just as it ever was—and here you two are, begrudging me compensation for everything I've done and continue to do."

"You agreed to the drawings for Cuddledown," snapped Carrie. "You wanted the view. You have the only beachfront house, Bess, and you have all Dad's approval and devotion. I'd think that would be enough for you. Lord knows it's impossible for the rest of us to get."

"You choose not to have it," said Bess. "You choose Ed; you choose to live with him. You choose to bring Gat here every summer, when you know he's not one of us. You know the way Dad thinks, and you not only keep running around with Ed, you bring his nephew here and parade him around like a defiant little girl with a forbidden toy. Your eyes have been wide open all the time."

"Shut up about Ed!" cried Carrie. "Just shut up, shut up."

There was a slap—Carrie hit Bess across the mouth.

Bess left. Slamming doors.

Mummy left, too.

Gat and I sat on the floor of the pantry, holding hands. Trying not to breathe, trying not to move while Carrie put the glasses in the dishwasher.

67

A COUPLE DAYS later, Granddad called Johnny into his Clairmont study. Asked Johnny to do him a favor.

Johnny said no.

Granddad said he would empty Johnny's college fund if Johnny didn't do it.

Johnny said he wasn't interfering in his mother's love life and he would bloody well work his way through community college, then.

Granddad called Thatcher.

Johnny told Carrie.

Carrie asked Gat to stop coming to supper at Clairmont. "It's riling Harris up," she said. "It would be better for all of us if you just made some macaroni at Red Gate, or I can have Johnny bring you a plate. You understand, don't you? Just until everything gets sorted out."

Gat did not understand.

Johnny didn't, either.

All of us Liars stopped coming to meals.

Soon after, Bess told Mirren to push Granddad harder about Windemere. She was to take Bonnie, Liberty, and Taft with her to talk with him in his study. They were the future of this family, Mirren was to say. Johnny and Cady didn't have the math grades for Harvard, while Mirren did. Mirren was the business-minded one, the heir to all Granddad stood for. Johnny and Cady were too frivolous. And look at these beautiful littles: the pretty blond twins, the freckle-faced Taft. They were Sinclairs, through and through.

Say all that, said Bess. But Mirren would not.

Bess took her phone, her laptop, and her allowance.

Mirren would not.

One evening Mummy asked about me and Gat. "Granddad knows something is going on with you two. He isn't happy."

I told her I was in love.

She said don't be silly. "You're risking the future," she said. "Our house. Your education. For what?"

"Love."

"A summer fling. Leave the boy alone."

"No."

"Love doesn't last, Cady. You know that."

"I don't."

"Well, believe me, it doesn't."

"We're not you and Dad," I said. "We're not."

Mummy crossed her arms. "Grow up, Cadence. See the world as it is, not as you wish it would be."

I looked at her. My lovely, tall mother with her pretty coil of hair and her hard, bitter mouth. Her veins were never open. Her heart never leapt out to flop helplessly on the lawn. She never melted into puddles. She was normal. Always. At any cost.

"For the health of our family," she said eventually, "you are to break it off."

"I won't."

"You must. And when you're done, make sure Granddad knows. Tell him it's nothing and tell him it never *was* anything. Tell him he shouldn't worry about that boy again and then talk to him about Harvard and tennis team and the future you have in front of you. Do you understand me?"

I did not and I would not.

I ran out of the house and into Gat's arms.

I bled on him and he didn't mind.

LATE THAT NIGHT, Mirren, Gat, Johnny, and I went down to the toolshed behind Clairmont. We found hammers. There were only two, so Gat carried a wrench and I carried a pair of heavy garden shears.

We collected the ivory goose from Clairmont, the elephants from Windemere, the monkeys from Red Gate, and the toad from Cuddledown. We brought them down to the dock in the dark and smashed them with the hammers and the wrench and the shears until the ivory was nothing but powder.

Gat ducked a bucket into the cold seawater and rinsed the dock clean.

68

WE THOUGHT.
    We talked.
    What if, we said,
    what if
    in another universe,
    a split reality,
    God reached out his finger and
    lightning struck the Clairmont house?
    What if

God sent it up in flames?

Thus he would punish the greedy, the petty, the prejudiced, the normal, the unkind.

They would repent of their deeds.

And after that, learn to love one another again.

Open their souls. Open their veins. Wipe off their smiles.

Be a family. Stay a family.

It wasn't religious, the way we thought of it.

And yet it was.

Punishment.

Purification through flames.

Or both.

69

NEXT DAY, LATE July of summer fifteen, there was a lunch at Clairmont. Another lunch like all the other lunches, set out on the big table. More tears.

The voices were so loud that we Liars came up the walkway from Red Gate and stood at the foot of the garden, listening.

"I have to earn your love every day, Dad," Mummy slurred. "And most days I fail. It's not fucking fair. Carrie gets the pearls, Bess gets the Boston house, Bess gets Windemere. Carrie has Johnny and you'll give him Clairmont, I know you will. I'll be left alone with nothing, nothing, even though Cady's supposed to be the one. The first, you always said."

Granddad stood from his seat at the head of the table. "Penelope."

"I'll take her away, do you hear me? I'll take Cady away and you won't see her again."

Granddad's voice boomed across the yard. "This is the United States of America," he said. "You don't seem to understand that, Penny, so let me explain. In America, here is how we operate: We work for what we want, and we get ahead. We never take no for answer, and we deserve the rewards of our perseverance. Will, Taft, are you listening?"

The little boys nodded, chins quivering. Granddad continued: "We Sinclairs are a grand, old family. That is something to be proud of. Our traditions and values form the bedrock on which future generations stand. This island is our home, as it was my father's and my grandfather's before him. And yet the three of you women, with these divorces, broken homes, this disrespect for tradition, this lack of a work ethic, you have done nothing but disappoint an old man who thought he raised you right."

"Dad, please," said Bess.

"Be quiet!" thundered Granddad. "You cannot expect me to accept your disregard for the values of this family and reward you and your children with financial security. You cannot, any of you, expect this. And yet, day after day, I see that you do. I will no longer tolerate it."

Bess crumpled in tears.

Carrie grabbed Will by the elbow and walked toward the dock.

Mummy threw her wineglass against the side of Clairmont house.

70

"WHAT HAPPENED THEN?" I ask Johnny. We are still lying on the floor of Cuddledown, early in the morning. Summer seventeen.

"You don't remember?" he says.

"No."

"People started leaving the island. Carrie took Will to a hotel in Edgartown and asked me and Gat to follow her as soon as we'd packed everything. The staff departed at eight. Your mother went to see that friend of hers on the Vineyard—"

"Alice?"

"Yes, Alice came and got her, but you wouldn't leave, and finally she had to go without you. Granddad took off for the mainland. And then we decided about the fire."

"We planned it out," I say.

"We did. We convinced Bess to take the big boat and all the littles to see a movie on the Vineyard."

As Johnny talks, the memories form. I fill in details he hasn't spoken aloud.

"When they left we drank the wine they'd left corked in the fridge," says Johnny. "Four open bottles. And Gat was so angry—"

"He was right," I say.

Johnny turns his face and speaks into the floor again. "Because he wasn't coming back. If my mom married Ed, they'd be cut off. And if my mom left Ed, Gat wouldn't be connected to our family anymore."

"Clairmont was like the symbol of everything that was wrong." It is Mirren's voice. She came in so quietly I didn't hear. She is now lying on the floor next to Johnny, holding his other hand.

"The seat of the patriarchy," says Gat. I didn't hear him come in, either. He lies down next to me.

"You're such an ass, Gat," says Johnny kindly. "You always say patriarchy."

"It's what I mean."

"You sneak it in whenever you can. Patriarchy on toast. Patriarchy in my pants. Patriarchy with a squeeze of lemon."

"Clairmont seemed like the seat of the patriarchy," repeats Gat. "And yes, we were stupid drunk, and yes, we thought they'd rip the family apart and I would never come here again. We figured if the house was gone, and the paperwork and data inside it gone, and all the objects they fought about gone, the power would be gone."

"We could be a family," says Mirren.

"It was like a purification," says Gat.

"She remembers we set a fire is all," says Johnny, his voice suddenly loud.

"And some other things," I add, sitting up and looking at the Liars in the morning light. "Things are coming back as you're filling me in."

"We are telling you all the stuff that happened before we set the fire," says Johnny, still loud.

"Yes," says Mirren.

"We set a fire," I say, in wonder. "We didn't sob and bleed; we did something instead. Made a change."

"Kind of," says Mirren.

"Are you kidding? We burned that fucking palace to the ground."

71

AFTER THE AUNTIES and Granddad quarreled, I was crying.

Gat was crying, too.

He was going to leave the island and I'd never see him again. He would never see me.

Gat, my Gat.

I had never cried with anyone before. At the same time.

He cried like a man, not like a boy. Not like he was frustrated or hadn't gotten his way, but like life was bitter. Like his wounds couldn't be healed.

I wanted to heal them for him.

We ran down to the tiny beach alone. I clung to him and we sat together in the sand, and for once he had nothing to say. No analysis, no questions.

Finally I said something about

what if

what if

we took it into our own hands?

And Gat said,

How?

And I said something about

what if

what if

they could stop fighting?

We have something to save.

And Gat said,

Yes. You and me and Mirren and Johnny, yes, we do.

But of course we can always see each other, the four of us.

Next year we can drive.

There is always the phone.

But here, I said. This.

Yes, here, he said. This.

You and me.

I said something about

what if

what if

we could somehow stop being

the Beautiful Sinclair Family and just be a family?

What if we could stop being

different colors, different backgrounds, and just be in love?

What if we could force everyone to change?

Force them.

You want to play God, Gat said.

I want to take action, I said. There is always the phone, he said.

But what about here? I said. This.

Yes, here, he said. This.

Gat was my love, my first and only. How could I let him go?

He was a person who couldn't fake a smile but smiled often. He wrapped my wrists in white gauze and believed wounds needed attention. He wrote on his hands and asked me my thoughts. His mind was restless, relentless. He didn't believe in God anymore and yet he still wished that God would help him.

And now he was mine and I said we should not let our love be threatened.

We should not let the family fall apart.

We should not accept an evil we can change.

We would stand up against it, would we not?

Yes. We should.

We would be heroes, even.

GAT AND I talked to Mirren and Johnny.

Convinced them to take action.

We told each other

over and over: do what you are afraid to do.

We told each other.

Over and over, we said it.

We told each other

we were right.

72

THE PLAN WAS simple. We would find the spare jugs of gas, the ones kept in the shed for the motorboats. There were newspapers and cardboard in the mudroom: we'd build piles of recycling and soak those in gasoline. We'd soak the wood floors as well. Stand back. Light a paper towel roll and throw it. Easy.

We would light every floor, every room, if possible, to make sure Clairmont burned completely. Gat in the basement, me on the ground floor, Johnny on the second, and Mirren on top.

"The fire department arrived really late," says Mirren.

"Two fire departments," says Johnny. "Woods Hole and Martha's Vineyard."

"We were counting on that," I say, realizing.

"We planned to call for help," says Johnny. "Of course someone had to call or it would look like arson. We were going to say we were all down at Cuddledown, watching a movie, and you know how the trees surround it. You can't see the other houses unless you go on the roof. So it made sense that no one would have called."

"Those fire departments are mainly volunteers," says Gat. "No one had a clue. Old wood house. Tinderbox."

"If the aunts and Granddad suspected us, they'd never prosecute," adds Johnny. "It was easy to bank on that."

Of course they wouldn't prosecute.

No one here is a criminal.

No one is an addict.

No one is a failure.

I feel a thrill at what we have done.

My full name is Cadence Sinclair Eastman, and contrary to the expectations of the beautiful family in which I was raised, I am an arsonist.

A visionary, a heroine, a rebel.

The kind of person who changes history.

A criminal.

But if I am a criminal, am I, then, an addict? Am I, then, a failure?

My mind is playing with twists of meaning as it always does. "We made it happen," I say.

"Depends on what you think it is," says Mirren.

"We saved the family. They started over."

"Aunt Carrie's wandering the island at night," says Mirren. "My mother's scrubbing clean sinks till her hands are raw. Penny watches you sleep and writes down what you eat. They drink a fuckload. They're getting drunk until the tears roll down their faces."

"When are you even at New Clairmont to see that?" I say.

"I get up there now and then," Mirren says. "You think we solved everything, Cady, but I think it was—"

"We're here," I persist. "Without that fire, we wouldn't be here. That's what I'm saying."

"Okay."

"Granddad held so much power," I say. "And now he doesn't. We changed an evil we saw in the world."

I understand so much that wasn't clear before. My tea is warm, the Liars are beautiful, Cuddledown is beautiful. It doesn't matter if there are stains on the wall. It doesn't matter if I have headaches or Mirren is sick. It doesn't matter if Will has nightmares and Gat hates himself. We have committed the perfect crime.

"Granddad only lacks power because he's demented," says Mirren. "He would still torture everybody if he could."

"I don't agree with you," says Gat. "New Clairmont seems like a punishment to me."

"What?" she asks.

"A self-punishment. He built himself a home that isn't a home. It's deliberately uncomfortable."

"Why would he do that?" I ask.

"Why did you give away all your belongings?" Gat asks.

He is staring at me. They are all staring at me.

"To be charitable," I answer. "To do some good in the world."

There is a strange silence.

"I hate clutter," I say.

No one laughs. I don't know how this conversation came to be all about me.

None of the Liars speaks for a long time. Then Johnny says, "Don't push it, Gat," and Gat says, "I'm glad you remember the fire, Cadence," and I say, "Yah, well, some of it," and Mirren says she doesn't feel well and goes back to bed.

The boys and I lie on the kitchen floor and stare at the ceiling for a while longer, until I realize, with some embarrassment, that they have both fallen asleep.

73

I FIND MY mother on the Windemere porch with the goldens. She is crocheting a scarf of pale blue wool.

"You're always at Cuddledown," Mummy complains. "It's not good to be down there all the time. Carrie went yesterday, looking for something, and she said it was filthy. What have you been doing?"

"Nothing. Sorry about the mess."

"If it's really dirty we can't ask Ginny to clean it. You know that, right? It's not fair to her. And Bess will have a fit if she sees it."

I don't want anyone coming into Cuddledown. I want it just

for us. "Don't worry." I sit down and pat Bosh on his sweet yellow head. "Listen, Mummy?"

"Yes?"

"Why did you tell the family not to talk to me about the fire?"

She puts down her yarn and looks at me for a long time. "You remember the fire?"

"Last night, it came rushing back. I don't remember all of it, but yeah. I remember it happened. I remember you all argued. And everyone left the island. I remember I was here with Gat, Mirren, and Johnny."

"Do you remember anything else?"

"What the sky looked like. With the flames. The smell of the smoke."

If Mummy thinks I am in any way at fault, she will never, ever, ask me. I know she won't.

She doesn't want to know.

I changed the course of her life. I changed the fate of the family. The Liars and I.

It was a horrible thing to do. Maybe. But it was something. It wasn't sitting by, complaining. I am a more powerful person than my mother will ever know. I have trespassed against her and helped her, too.

She strokes my hair. So cloying. I pull back. "That's all?" she asks.

"Why doesn't anyone talk to me about it?" I repeat.

"Because of your—because of—" Mummy stops, looking for words. "Because of your pain."

"Because I have headaches, because I can't remember my accident, I can't handle the idea that Clairmont burned down?"

"The doctors told me not to add stress to your life," she says. "They said the fire might have triggered the headaches, whether it was smoke inhalation or—or fear," she finishes lamely.

"I'm not a child," I say. "I can be trusted to know basic information about our family. All summer I've been working to remember my accident, and what happened right before. Why not tell me, Mummy?"

"I did tell you. Two years ago. I told you over and over, but you never remembered it the next day. And when I talked to the doctor, he said I shouldn't keep upsetting you that way, shouldn't keep pushing you."

"You live with me!" I cry. "Don't you have any faith in your own judgment over that of some doctor who barely knows me?"

"He's an expert."

"What makes you think I'd want my whole extended family keeping secrets from me—even the twins, even Will and Taft, for God's sake—rather than know what happened? What makes you think I am so fragile I can't even know simple facts?"

"You seem that fragile to me," says Mummy. "And to be honest, I haven't been sure I could handle your reaction."

"You can't even imagine how insulting that is."

"I love you," she says.

I can't look at her pitying, self-justifying face any longer.

74

MIRREN IS IN my room when I open the door. She is sitting at my desk with her hand on my laptop.

"I wonder if I could read the emails you sent me last year," she says. "Do you have them on your computer?"

"Yeah."

"I never read them," she says. "At the start of the summer I pretended I did, but I never even opened them."

"Why not?"

"I just didn't," she says. "I thought it didn't matter, but now I think it does. And look!" She makes her voice light. "I even left the house to do it!"

I swallow as much anger as I can. "I understand not writing back, but why wouldn't you even read my emails?"

"I know," Mirren says. "It sucks and I'm a horrible wench. Please, will you let me read them now?"

I open the laptop. Do a search and find all the notes addressed to her.

There are twenty-eight. I read over her shoulder. Most of them are charming, darling emails from a person supposedly without headaches.

Mirren!

Tomorrow I leave for Europe with my cheating father, who is, as you know, also deeply boring. Wish me luck and know that I wish I were spending the summer on Beechwood with you. And Johnny. And even Gat.

I know, I know. I should be over it.

I am over it.

I am.

Off to Marbella to meet attractive Spanish boys, so there.

I wonder if I can make Dad eat the most disgusting foods of every country we visit, as penance for his running off to Colorado.

I bet I can. If he really loves me, he will eat frogs and kidneys and chocolate-covered ants.

/Cadence

THAT'S HOW MOST of them go. But a few of the emails are neither charming nor darling. Those ones are pitiful and true.

Mirren.

Vermont winter. Dark, dark.

Mummy keeps looking at me while I sleep.

My head hurts all the time. I don't know what to do to make it stop. The pills don't work. Someone is splitting through the top of my head with an axe, a messy axe that won't make a clean cut through my skull. Whoever wields it has to hack away at my head, coming down over and over, but not always right in the same place. I have multiple wounds.

I dream sometimes that the person wielding the axe is Granddad.

Other times, the person is me.

Other times, the person is Gat.

188

Sorry to sound crazy. My hands are shaky as I type this and the screen is too bright.

I want to die, sometimes, my head hurts so much. I keep writing you all my brightest thoughts but I never say the dark ones, even though I think them all the time. So I am saying them now. Even if you do not answer, I will know somebody heard them, and that, at least, is something.

/Cadence

WE READ ALL twenty-eight emails. When she is finished, Mirren kisses me on the cheek. "I can't even say sorry," she tells me. "There is not even a Scrabble word for how bad I feel."

Then she is gone.

75

I BRING MY laptop to the bed and create a document. I take down my graph-paper notes and begin typing those and all my new memories, fast and with a thousand errors. I fill in gaps with guesses where I don't have actual recall.

The Sinclair Center for Socialization and Snacks.

You won't see that boyfriend of yours again.

He wants me to stay the hell away from you.

We adore Windemere, don't we, Cady?

Aunt Carrie, crying in Johnny's Windbreaker.

Gat throwing balls for the dogs on the tennis court.

Oh God, oh God, oh God.

The dogs.

The fucking dogs.

Fatima and Prince Philip.

The goldens died in that fire.

I know it now, and it is my fault. They were such naughty dogs, not like Bosh, Grendel, and Poppy, whom Mummy trained. Fatima and Prince Philip ate starfish on the shore, then vomited them up in the living room. They shook water from their shaggy fur, snarfled people's picnic lunches, chewed Frisbees into hunks of unusable plastic. They loved tennis balls and would go down to the court and slime any that had been left around. They would not sit when told. They begged at the table.

When the fire caught, the dogs were in one of the guest bedrooms. Granddad often closed them in upstairs while Clairmont was empty, or at night. That way they wouldn't eat people's boots or howl at the screen door.

Granddad had shut them up before he left the island.

And we hadn't thought of them.

I had killed those dogs. It was I who lived with dogs, I who knew where Prince Philip and Fatima slept. The rest of the Liars didn't think about the goldens—not very much, anyway. Not like I did.

They had burned to death. How could I have forgotten them like that? How could I have been so wrapped up in my own stupid criminal exercise, the thrill of it, my own anger at the aunties and Granddad—

Fatima and Prince Philip, burning. Sniffing at the hot door, breathing in smoke, wagging their tails hopefully, waiting for someone to come and get them, barking.

What a horrible death for those poor, dear, naughty dogs.

190

76

I RUN OUT of Windemere. It is dark out now, nearly time for supper. My feelings leak out my eyes, crumpling my face, heave through my frame as I imagine the dogs, hoping for a rescue, staring at the door as the smoke billows in.

Where to go? I cannot face the Liars at Cuddledown. Red Gate might have Will or Aunt Carrie. The island is so fucking small, actually, there's nowhere to go. I am trapped on this island, where I killed those poor, poor dogs.

All my bravado from this morning,

the power,

the perfect crime,

taking down the patriarchy,

the way we Liars saved the summer idyll and made it better,

the way we kept our family together by destroying some part of it—

all that is delusional.

The dogs are dead,

the stupid, lovely dogs,

the dogs I could have saved,

innocent dogs whose faces lit when you snuck them a bit of hamburger

or even said their names;

dogs who loved to go on boats,

who ran free all day on muddy paws.

What kind of person takes action without thinking about

who might be locked in an upstairs room, trusting the people who have always kept them safe and loved them?

I am sobbing these strange, silent sobs, standing on the walkway between Windemere and Red Gate. My face is soaked, my chest is contracting. I stumble back home.

Gat is on the steps.

77

HE JUMPS UP when he sees me and wraps his arms around me. I sob into his shoulder and tuck my arms under his jacket and around his waist.

He doesn't ask what's wrong until I tell him.

"The dogs," I say finally. "We killed the dogs."

He is quiet for a moment. Then, "Yeah."

I don't speak again until my body stops shaking.

"Let's sit down," Gat says.

We settle on the porch steps. Gat rests his head against mine.

"I loved those dogs," I say.

"We all did."

"I—" I choke on my words. "I don't think I should talk about it anymore or I'll start crying again."

"All right."

We sit for a while longer.

"Is that everything?" Gat asks.

"What?"

"Everything you were crying about?"

"God forbid there's more."

He is silent.

And still silent.

"Oh hell, there is more," I say, and my chest feels hollow and iced.

"Yeah," says Gat. "There is more."

"More that people aren't telling me. More that Mummy would rather I didn't remember."

He takes a moment to think. "I think we're telling you, but you can't hear it. You've been sick, Cadence."

"You're not telling me directly," I say.

"No."

"Why the hell not?"

"Penny said it was best. And—well, with all of us being here, I had faith that you'd remember." He takes his arm off my shoulder and wraps his hands around his knees.

Gat, my Gat.

He is contemplation and enthusiasm. Ambition and strong coffee. I love the lids of his brown eyes, his smooth dark skin, his lower lip that pushes out. His mind. His mind.

I kiss his cheek. "I remember more about us than I used to," I tell him. "I remember you and me kissing at the door of the mudroom before it all went so wrong. You and me on the tennis court talking about Ed proposing to Carrie. On the perimeter at the flat rock, where no one could see us. And down on the tiny beach, talking about setting the fire."

He nods.

"But I still don't remember what went wrong," I say. "Why we weren't together when I got hurt. Did we have an argument? Did I do something? Did you go back to Raquel?" I cannot look him in the eyes. "I think I deserve an honest answer, even if whatever's between us now isn't going to last."

Gat's face crumples and he hides it in his hands. "I don't know what to do," he says. "I don't know what I'm supposed to do."

"Just tell me," I say.

"I can't stay here with you," he says. "I have to go back to Cuddledown."

"Why?"

"I have to," he says, standing up and walking. Then he stops and turns. "I messed everything up. I'm so sorry, Cady. I am so, so sorry." He is crying again. "I shouldn't have kissed you, or made you a tire swing, or given you roses. I shouldn't have told you how beautiful you are."

"I wanted you to."

"I know, but I should have stayed away. It's fucked up that I did all that. I'm sorry."

"Come back here," I say, but when he doesn't move, I go to him. Put my hands on his neck and my cheek against his. I kiss him hard so he knows I mean it. His mouth is so soft and he's just the best person I know, the best person I've ever known, no matter what bad things have happened between us and no matter what happens after this. "I love you," I whisper.

He pulls back. "This is what I'm talking about. I'm sorry. I just wanted to see you."

He turns around and is lost in the dark.

78

THE HOSPITAL ON Martha's Vineyard. Summer fifteen, after my accident.

I was lying in a bed under blue sheets. You would think hospital sheets would be white, but these were blue. The room was hot. I had an IV in one arm.

Mummy and Granddad were staring down at me. Granddad was holding a box of Edgartown fudge he'd brought as a gift.

It was touching that he remembered I like the Edgartown fudge.

I was listening to music with ear buds in my ears, so I couldn't hear what the adults were saying. Mummy was crying.

Granddad opened the fudge, broke off a piece, and offered it to me.

The song:

> *Our youth is wasted*
> *We will not waste it*
> *Remember my name*
> *'Cause we made history*
> *Na na na na, na na na*

I LIFTED MY hand to take out the ear buds. The hand I saw was bandaged.

Both my hands were bandaged.

And my feet. I could feel the tape on them, beneath the blue sheets.

My hands and feet were bandaged, because they were burned.

79

ONCE UPON A *time there was a king who had three beautiful daughters.*

No, no, wait.

Once upon a time there were three bears who lived in a wee house in the woods.

Once upon a time there were three billy goats who lived near a bridge.

Once upon a time there were three soldiers, tramping together down the roads after the war.

Once upon a time there were three little pigs.

Once upon a time there were three brothers.

No, this is it. This is the variation I want.

Once upon a time there were three beautiful children, two boys and a girl. When each baby was born, the parents rejoiced, the heavens rejoiced, even the fairies rejoiced. The fairies came to christening parties and gave the babies magical gifts.

Bounce, effort, and snark.

Contemplation and enthusiasm. Ambition and strong coffee.

Sugar, curiosity, and rain.

And yet, there was a witch.

There is always a witch.

This witch was the same age as the beautiful children, and as she and they grew, she was jealous of the girl, and jealous of the boys, too. They were blessed with all these fairy gifts, gifts the witch had been denied at her own christening.

The eldest boy was strong and fast, capable and handsome. Though it's true, he was exceptionally short.

The next boy was studious and open-hearted. Though it's true, he was an outsider.

And the girl was witty, generous, and ethical. Though it's true, she felt powerless.

The witch, she was none of these things, for her parents had angered the fairies. No gifts were ever bestowed upon her. She was lonely. Her only strength was her dark and ugly magic.

She confused being spartan with being charitable, and gave away her possessions without truly doing good with them.

She confused being sick with being brave, and suffered agonies while imagining she merited praise for it.

She confused wit with intelligence, and made people laugh rather than lightening their hearts or making them think.

Her magic was all she had, and she used it to destroy what she most admired. She visited each young person in turn on their tenth birthday, but did not harm them outright. The protection of some kind fairy—the lilac fairy, perhaps—prevented her from doing so.

What she did instead was curse them.

"When you are sixteen," proclaimed the witch in a rage of jealousy, "when we are all sixteen," she told these beautiful children, "you shall prick your finger on a spindle—no, you shall strike a match—yes, you will strike a match and die in its flame."

The parents of the beautiful children were frightened of the curse, and tried, as people will do, to avoid it. They moved

197

hemselves and the children far away, to a castle on a wind-swept island. A castle where there were no matches.

There, surely, they would be safe.

There, surely, the witch would never find them.

But find them she did. And when they were fifteen, these beautiful children, just before their sixteenth birthdays and when their nervous parents were not yet expecting it, the jealous witch brought her toxic, hateful self into their lives in the shape of a blond maiden.

The maiden befriended the beautiful children. She kissed them and took them on boat rides and brought them fudge and told them stories.

Then she gave them a box of matches.

The children were entranced, for at nearly sixteen they had never seen fire.

Go on, strike, said the witch, smiling. Fire is beautiful. Nothing bad will happen.

Go on, she said, the flames will cleanse your souls.

Go on, she said, for you are independent thinkers.

Go on, she said. What is this life we lead, if you do not take action?

And they listened.

They took the matches from her and they struck them. The witch watched their beauty burn,

> *their bounce,*
> *their intelligence,*
> *their wit,*
> *their open hearts,*
> *their charm,*
> *their dreams for the future.*

She watched it all disappear in smoke.

PART FIVE

Truth

80

HERE IS THE truth about the Beautiful Sinclair Family. At least, the truth as Granddad knows it. The truth he was careful to keep out of all newspapers.

One night, two summers ago, on a warm July evening,

Gatwick Matthew Patil,

Mirren Sinclair Sheffield,

and

Jonathan Sinclair Dennis

perished in a house fire thought to be caused by a jug of motorboat fuel that overturned in the mudroom. The house in question burned to the ground before the neighboring fire departments arrived on the scene.

Cadence Sinclair Eastman was present on the island at the time of the fire but did not notice it until it was well under way. The conflagration prevented her from entering the building when she realized there were people and animals trapped inside. She sustained burns to the hands and feet in her rescue attempts. Then she ran to another home on the island and telephoned the fire department.

When help finally arrived, Miss Eastman was found on the tiny beach, half underwater and curled into a ball. She was unable to answer questions about what happened and appeared to have suffered a head injury. She had to be heavily sedated for many days following the accident.

Harris Sinclair, owner of the island, declined any formal

investigation of the fire's origin. Many of the surrounding trees were decimated.

Funerals were held for

Gatwick Matthew Patil,

Mirren Sinclair Sheffield,

and

Jonathan Sinclair Dennis

in their hometowns of Cambridge and New York City.

Cadence Sinclair Eastman was not well enough to attend.

The following summer, the Sinclair family returned to Beechwood Island. They fell apart. They mourned. They drank a lot.

Then they built a new house on the ashes of the old.

Cadence Sinclair Eastman had no memory of the events surrounding the fire, no memory of it ever happening. Her burns healed quickly but she exhibited selective amnesia regarding the events of the previous summer. She persisted in believing she had injured her head while swimming. Doctors presumed her crippling migraine headaches were caused by unacknowledged grief and guilt. She was heavily medicated and extremely fragile both physically and mentally.

These same doctors advised Cadence's mother to stop explaining the tragedy if Cadence could not recall it herself. It was too much to be told of the trauma fresh each day. Let her remember in her own time. She should not return to Beechwood Island until she'd had significant time to heal. In fact, any measures possible should be taken to keep her from the island in the year immediately after the accident.

Cadence displayed a disquieting desire to rid herself of all unnecessary possessions, even things of sentimental value, almost as if doing penance for past crimes. She darkened her hair and took to dressing very simply. Her mother sought profes-

sional advice about Cadence's behavior and was advised tha
appeared a normal part of the grieving process.

In the second year after the accident, the family began to
recover. Cadence was once again attending school after many
long absences. Eventually, the girl expressed a desire to return
to Beechwood Island. The doctors and other family members
agreed: it might be good for her to do just that.

On the island, perhaps, she would finish healing.

81

REMEMBER, DON'T GET your feet wet. Or your clothes.

Soak the linen cupboards, the towels, the floors, the books,
and the beds.

Remember, move the gas can away from your kindling so
you can grab it.

See it catch, see it burn. Then run. Use the kitchen stairwell
and exit out the mudroom door.

Remember, take your gas can with you and return it to the
boathouse.

See you at Cuddledown. We'll put our clothes in the washer
there, change, then go and watch the blaze before we call the
fire departments.

Those are the last words I said to any of them. Johnny and
Mirren went to the top two floors of Clairmont carrying cans
of gas and bags of old newspapers for kindling.

I kissed Gat before he went down to the basement. "See you
in a better world," he said to me, and I laughed.

We were a bit drunk. We'd been at the aunties' leftover wine since they left the island. The alcohol made me feel giddy and powerful until I stood in the kitchen alone. Then I felt dizzy and nauseated.

The house was cold. It felt like something that deserved to be destroyed. It was filled with objects over which the aunties fought. Valuable art, china, photographs. All of them fueled family anger. I hit my fist against the kitchen portrait of Mummy, Carrie, and Bess as children, grinning for the camera. The glass on it shattered and I stumbled back.

The wine was muddling my head now. I wasn't used to it.

The gas can in one hand and the bag of kindling in the other, I decided to get this done as fast as possible. I doused the kitchen first, then the pantry. I did the dining room and was soaking the living room couches when I realized I should have started at the end of the house farthest from the mudroom door. That was our exit. I should have done the kitchen last so I could run out without wetting my feet with gasoline.

Stupid.

The formal door that opened onto the front porch from the living room was soaked already, but there was a small back door, too. It was by Granddad's study and led to the walkway down to the staff building. I would use that.

I doused part of the hall and then the craft room, feeling a wave of sorrow for the ruin of Gran's beautiful cotton prints and colorful yarns. She would have hated what I was doing. She loved her fabrics, her old sewing machine, her pretty, pretty objects.

Stupid again. I had soaked my espadrilles in fuel.

All right. Stay calm. I'd wear them until I was done and then toss them into the fire behind me as I ran outside.

In Granddad's study I stood on the desk, splashing bookshelves up to the ceiling, holding the gas can far away from me. There was a fair amount of gas left, and this was my last room, so I soaked the books heavily.

Then I wet the floor, piled the kindling on it, and backed into the small foyer that led to the rear door. I got my shoes off and threw them onto the stack of magazines. I stepped onto a square of dry floor and set the gas can down. Pulled a matchbook from the pocket of my jeans and lit my paper towel roll.

I threw the flaming roll into the kindling and watched it light. It caught, and grew, and spread. Through the double-wide study doors, I saw a line of flame zip down the hallway on one side and into the living room on the other. The couch lit up.

Then, before me, the bookshelves burst into flames, the gas-soaked paper burning quicker than anything else. Suddenly the ceiling was alight. I couldn't look away. The flames were terrible. Unearthly.

Then someone screamed.

And screamed again.

It was coming from the room directly above me, a bedroom. Johnny was working on the second floor. I had lit the study, and the study had burned faster than anywhere else. The fire was rising, and Johnny wasn't out.

Oh no, oh no, oh no. I threw myself at the back door but found it heavily bolted. My hands were slippery with gas. The metal was hot already. I flipped the bolts—one, two, three—but something went wrong and the door stuck.

Another scream.

I tried the bolts again. Failed. Gave up.

I covered my mouth and nose with my hands and ran through the burning study and down the flaming hallway into the kitchen. The room wasn't lit yet, thank God. I rushed across the wet floor toward the mudroom door.

Stumbled, skidded, and fell, soaking myself in the puddles of gasoline.

The hems of my jeans were burning from my run through the study. The flames licked out to the gas on the kitchen floor and streaked across to the wooden farmhouse cabinetry and Gran's cheery dish towels. Fire zipped across the mudroom exit in front of me and I could see my jeans were now alight as well, from knee to ankle. I hurled myself toward the mudroom door, running through flames.

"Get out!" I yelled, though I doubted anyone could hear me. "Get out now!"

Outside I threw myself onto the grass. Rolled until my pants stopped burning.

I could see already that the top two floors of Clairmont were glowing with heat, and my own ground floor was fully alight. The basement level, I couldn't tell.

"Gat? Johnny? Mirren? Where are you?"

No answer.

Holding down panic, I told myself they must be out by now. Calm down. It would all be okay. It had to.

"Where are you?" I yelled again, beginning to run.

Again, no answer.

They were likely at the boathouse, dropping their gas cans. It wasn't far, and I ran, calling their names as loud as I could. My bare feet hit the wooden walkway with a strange echo.

The door was closed. I yanked it open. "Gat! Johnny? Mirren!"

No one there, but they could already be at Cuddledown, couldn't they? Wondering what was taking me so long.

A walkway stretches from the boathouse past the tennis courts and over to Cuddledown. I ran again, the island strangely hushed in the dark. I told myself over and over: They will be there. Waiting for me. Worrying about me.

We will laugh because we're all safe. We will soak my burns in ice water and feel all kinds of lucky.

We will.

But as I came upon it, I saw the house was dark.

No one waited there.

I tore back to Clairmont, and when it came into view it was burning, bottom to top. The turret room was lit, the bedrooms were lit, the windows of the basement glowed orange. Everything hot.

I ran to the mudroom entry and pulled the door. Smoke billowed out. I pulled off my gas-soaked sweater and jeans, choking and gagging. I pushed my way in and entered the kitchen stairwell, heading toward the basement.

Halfway down the steps there was a wall of flames. A wall.

Gat wasn't out. And he wasn't coming.

I turned back and ran up toward Johnny and Mirren, but the wood was burning beneath my feet.

The banister lit up. The stairwell in front of me caved in, throwing sparks.

I reeled back.

I could not go up.

I could not save them.

There was nowhere

nowhere

nowhere

nowhere now to go

but down.

82

I REMEMBER THIS like I am living it as I sit on the steps of Windemere, still staring at the spot where Gat disappeared into the night. The realization of what I have done comes as a fog in my chest, cold, dark, and spreading. I grimace and hunch over. The icy fog runs from my chest through my back and up my neck. It shoots through my head and down my spine.

Cold, cold, remorse.

I shouldn't have soaked the kitchen first. I shouldn't have lit the fire in the study.

How stupid to wet the books so thoroughly. Anyone might have predicted how they would burn. Anyone.

We should have had a set time to light our kindling.

I might have insisted we stay together.

I should never have checked the boathouse.

Should never have run to Cuddledown.

If only I'd gone back to Clairmont faster, maybe I could have gotten Johnny out. Or warned Gat before the basement caught. Maybe I could have found the fire extinguishers and stopped the flames somehow.

Maybe, maybe.

If only, if only.

I wanted so much for us: a life free of constriction and prejudice. A life free to love and be loved.

And here, I have killed them.

My Liars, my darlings.

Killed them. My Mirren, my Johnny, my Gat.

This knowledge goes from my spine down my shoulders and through my fingertips. It turns them to ice. They chip and break, tiny pieces shattering on the Windemere steps. Cracks splinter up my arms and through my shoulders and the front of my neck. My face is frozen and fractured in a witch's snarl of grief. My throat is closed. I cannot make a sound.

Here I am frozen, when I deserve to burn.

I should have shut up about taking things into our own hands. I could have stayed silent. Compromised. Talking on the phone would have been fine. Soon we'd have driver's licenses. Soon we'd go to college and the beautiful Sinclair houses would seem far away and unimportant.

We could have been patient.

I could have been a voice of reason.

Maybe then, when we drank the aunties' wine, we'd have forgotten our ambitions. The drink would have made us sleepy. We'd have dozed off in front of the television set, angry and impotent, perhaps, but without setting fire to anything.

I can't take any of it back.

I crawl indoors and up to my bedroom on hands of cracked ice, trailing shards of my frozen body behind me. My heels, my kneecaps. Beneath the blankets, I shiver convulsively, pieces of me breaking off onto my pillow. Fingers. Teeth. Jawbone. Collarbone.

Finally, finally, the shivering stops. I begin to warm and melt.

I cry for my aunts, who lost their firstborn children.

For Will, who lost his brother.

For Liberty, Bonnie, and Taft, who lost their sister.

For Granddad, who saw not just his palace burn to the ground, but his grandchildren perish.

For the dogs, the poor naughty dogs.

I cry for the vain, thoughtless complaints I've made all summer. For my shameful self-pity. For my plans for the future.

I cry for all my possessions, given away. I miss my pillow, my books, my photographs. I shudder at my delusions of charity, at my shame masquerading as virtue, at lies I've told myself, punishments I've inflicted on myself, and punishments I've inflicted on my mother.

I cry with horror that all the family has been burdened by me, and even more with being the cause of so much grief.

We did not, after all, save the idyll. That is gone forever, if it ever existed. We have lost the innocence of it, of those days before we knew the extent of the aunts' rage, before Gran's death and Granddad's deterioration.

Before we became criminals. Before we became ghosts.

The aunties hug one another not because they are freed of the weight of Clairmont house and all it symbolized, but out of tragedy and empathy. Not because we freed them, but because we wrecked them, and they clung to one another in the face of horror.

Johnny. Johnny wanted to run a marathon. He wanted to go mile upon mile, proving his lungs would not give out. Proving he was the man Granddad wanted him to be, proving his strength, though he was so small.

His lungs filled with smoke. He has nothing to prove now. There is nothing to run for.

He wanted to own a car and eat fancy cakes he saw in bakery widows. He wanted to laugh big and own art and wear beautifully made clothes. Sweaters, scarves, wooly items with stripes. He wanted to make a tuna fish of Lego and hang it like a piece of taxidermy. He refused to be serious, he was infuriatingly unserious, but he was as committed to the things that mattered to him as anyone could possibly be. The running. Will and Carrie. The Liars. His sense of what was right. He gave up his college fund without a second thought, to stand up for his principles.

I think of Johnny's strong arms, the stripe of white sunblock on his nose, the time we were sick together from poison ivy and lay next to each other in the hammock, scratching. The time he built me and Mirren a dollhouse of cardboard and stones he'd found on the beach.

Jonathan Sinclair Dennis, you would have been a light in the dark for so many people.

You *have* been one. You have.

And I have let you down the worst possible way.

I cry for Mirren, who wanted to see the Congo. She didn't know how she wanted to live or what she believed yet; she was searching and knew she was drawn to that place. It will never be real to her now, never anything more than photographs and films and stories published for people's entertainment.

Mirren talked a lot about sexual intercourse but never had it. When we were younger, she and I would stay up late, sleeping together on the Windemere porch in sleeping bags, laughing and eating fudge. We fought over Barbie dolls and did each other's makeup and dreamed of love. Mirren will never have a wedding with yellow roses or a groom who loves her enough to wear a stupid yellow cummerbund.

She was irritable. And bossy. But always funny about it. It was easy to make her mad, and she was nearly always cross with Bess and annoyed with the twins—but then she'd fill with regret, moaning in agony over her own sharp tongue. She did love her family, loved all of them, and would read them books or help them make ice cream or give them pretty shells she had found.

She cannot make amends anymore.

She did not want to be like her mother. Not a princess, no. An explorer, a businesswoman, a Good Samaritan, an ice cream maker—something.

Something she will never be, because of me.

Mirren, I can't even say sorry. There is not even a Scrabble word for how bad I feel.

And Gat, my Gat.

He will never go to college. He had that hungry mind, constantly turning things over, looking not for answers but for understanding. He will never satisfy his curiosity, never finish the hundred best novels ever written, never be the great man he might have been.

He wanted to stop evil. He wanted to express his anger. He lived big, my brave Gat. He didn't shut up when people wanted him to, he made them listen—and then he listened in return. He refused to take things lightly, though he was always quick to laugh.

Oh, he made me laugh. And made me think, even when I didn't feel like thinking, even when I was too lazy to pay attention.

Gat let me bleed on him and bleed on him and bleed on him. He never minded. He wanted to know why I was bleeding. He wondered what he could do to heal the wound.

He will never eat chocolate again.

I loved him. I love him. As best I could. But he was right. I did not know him all the way. I will never see his apartment, eat his mother's cooking, meet his friends from school. I will never see the bedspread on his bed or the posters on his walls. I'll never know the diner where he got egg sandwiches in the morning or the corner where he double-locked his bike.

I don't even know if he bought egg sandwiches or hung posters. I don't know if he owned a bike or had a bedspread. I am only imagining the corner bike racks and the double locks, because I never went home with him, never saw his life, never knew that person Gat was when not on Beechwood Island.

His room must be empty by now. He has been dead two years.

We might have been.

We might have been.

I have lost you, Gat, because of how desperately, desperately I fell in love.

I think of my Liars burning, in their last few minutes, breathing smoke, their skin alight. How much it must have hurt.

Mirren's hair in flames. Johnny's body on the floor. Gat's hands, his fingertips burnt, his arms shriveling with fire.

On the backs of his hands, words. Left: *Gat*. Right: *Cadence*.

My handwriting.

I cry because I am the only one of us still alive. Because I will have to go through life without the Liars. Because they will have to go through whatever awaits them, without me.

Me, Gat, Johnny, and Mirren.

Mirren, Gat, Johnny, and me.

We have been here, this summer.

And we have not been here.

Yes, and no.

It is my fault, my fault, my fault—and yet they love me anyway. Despite the poor dogs, despite my stupidity and grandiosity, despite our crime. Despite my selfishness, despite my whining, despite my stupid dumb luck in being the only one left and my inability to appreciate it, when they—they have nothing. Nothing, anymore, but this last summer together.

They have said they love me.

I have felt it in Gat's kiss.

In Johnny's laugh.

Mirren shouted it across the sea, even.

I GUESS THAT is why they've been here.

I needed them.

83

MUMMY BANGS ON my door and calls my name.

I do not answer.

An hour later, she bangs again.

"Let me in, won't you?"

"Go away."

"Is it a migraine? Just tell me that."

"It isn't a migraine," I say. "It's something else."

"I love you, Cady," she says.

She says it all the time since I got sick, but only now do I see that what Mummy means is,

I love you in spite of my grief. Even though you are crazy.

I love you in spite of what I suspect you have done.

"You know we all love you, right?" she calls through the door. "Aunt Bess and Aunt Carrie and Granddad and everyone? Bess is making the blueberry pie you like. It'll be out in half an hour. You could have it for breakfast. I asked her."

I stand. Go to the door and open it a crack. "Tell Bess I say thank you," I say. "I just can't come right now."

"You've been crying," Mummy says.

"A little."

"I see."

"Sorry. I know you want me at the house for breakfast."

"You don't need to say you're sorry," Mummy tells me. "Really, you don't ever have to say it, Cady."

84

AS USUAL, NO one is visible at Cuddledown until my feet make sounds on the steps. Then Johnny appears at the door, stepping gingerly over the crushed glass. When he sees my face, he stops.

"You've remembered," he says.

I nod.

"You've remembered everything?"

"I didn't know if you would still be here," I say.

He reaches out to hold my hand. He feels warm and substantial, though he looks pale, washed out, bags under his eyes. And young.

He is only fifteen.

"We can't stay much longer," Johnny says. "It's getting harder and harder."

I nod.

"Mirren's got it the worst, but Gat and I are feeling it, too."

"Where will you go?"

"When we leave?"

"Uh-huh."

"Same place as when you're not here. Same place as we've been. It's like—" Johnny pauses, scratches his head. "It's like a rest. It's like nothing, in a way. And honestly, Cady, I love you, but I'm fucking tired. I just want to lie down and be done. All this happened a very long time ago, for me."

I look at him. "I'm so, so sorry, my dear old Johnny," I say, feeling the tears well behind my eyes.

"Not your fault," says Johnny. "I mean, we all did it, we all went crazy, we have to take responsibility. You shouldn't carry the weight of it," he says. "Be sad, be sorry—but don't shoulder it."

We go into the house and Mirren comes out of her bedroom. I realize she probably wasn't there until moments before I walked through the door. She hugs me. Her honey hair is dim and the edges of her mouth look dry and cracked. "I'm sorry I didn't do all of this better, Cady," she says. "I got one chance to be here, and I don't know, I drew it out, told so many lies."

"It's all right."

"I want to be an accepting person, but I am so full of leftover rage. I imagined I'd be saintly and wise, but instead I've been jealous of you, mad at the rest of my family. It's just messed up and now it's done," she says, burying her face in my shoulder.

I put my arms around her. "You were yourself, Mirren," I say. "I don't want anything else."

"I have to go now," she says. "I can't be here any longer. I'm going down to the sea."

No. Please.

Don't go. Don't leave me, Mirren, Mirren.

I need you.

That is what I want to say, to shout. But I do not.

And part of me wants to bleed across the great room floor or melt into a puddle of grief.

But I do not do that, either. I do not complain or ask for pity.

I cry instead. I cry and squeeze Mirren and kiss her on her warm cheek and try to memorize her face.

We hold hands as the three of us walk down to the tiny beach.

Gat is there, waiting for us. His profile against the lit sky. I will see it forever like that. He turns and smiles at me. Runs and picks me up, swinging me around as if there's something to celebrate. As if we are a happy couple, in love on the beach.

I am not sobbing anymore, but tears stream from my eyes without cease. Johnny takes off his button-down and hands it to me. "Wipe your snotface," he says kindly.

Mirren strips off her sundress and stands there in a bathing suit. "I can't believe you put on a bikini for this," says Gat, his arms still around me.

"Certifiable," adds Johnny.

"I love this bikini," says Mirren. "I got it in Edgartown, summer fifteen. Do you remember, Cady?"

And I find that I do.

We were desperately bored; the littles had rented bikes to go on this scenic ride to Oak Bluffs and we had no idea when they'd return. We had to wait and bring them back on the boat. So, whatever, we'd shopped for fudge, we'd looked at wind

, and finally we went into a tourist shop and tried on the ...est bathing suits we could find.

"It says *The Vineyard Is for Lovers* on the butt," I tell Johnny.

Mirren turns around, and indeed it does. "Blaze of glory and all that," she says, not without bitterness.

She walks over, kisses me on the cheek, and says, "Be a little kinder than you have to, Cady, and things will be all right."

"And never eat anything bigger than your ass!" yells Johnny. He gives me a quick hug and kicks off his shoes. The two of them wade into the sea.

I turn to Gat. "You going, too?"

He nods.

"I am so sorry, Gat," I say. "I am so, so sorry, and I will never be able to make it up to you."

He kisses me, and I can feel him shaking, and I wrap my arms around him like I could stop him from disappearing, like I could make this moment last, but his skin is cold and damp with tears and I know he is leaving.

It is good to be loved, even though it will not last.

It is good to know that once upon a time, there was Gat and me.

Then he takes off, and I cannot bear to be separate from him, and I think, this cannot be the end. It can't be true we won't ever be together again, not when our love is so real. The story is supposed to have a happy ending.

But no.

He is leaving me.

He is dead already, of course.

The story ended a long time ago.

Gat runs into the sea without looking back, plunging in, in all his clothes, diving underneath the small waves.

The Liars swim out, past the edge of the cove and into the open ocean. The sun is high in the sky and glints off the water, so bright, so bright. And then they dive—

or something—

or something—

and they are gone.

I am left, there on the southern tip of Beechwood Island. I am on the tiny beach, alone.

85

I SLEEP FOR what might be days. I can't get up.

I open my eyes, it's light out.

I open my eyes, it's dark.

Finally I stand. In the bathroom mirror, my hair is no longer black. It has faded to a rusty brown, with blond roots. My skin is freckled and my lips are sunburnt.

I am not sure who that girl in the mirror is.

Bosh, Grendel, and Poppy follow me out of the house, panting and wagging their tails. In the New Clairmont kitchen, the aunties are making sandwiches for a picnic lunch. Ginny is cleaning out the refrigerator. Ed is putting bottles of lemonade and ginger ale into a cooler.

Ed.

Hello, Ed.

He waves at me. Opens a bottle of ginger ale and gives it to Carrie. Rummages in the freezer for another bag of ice.

Bonnie is reading and Liberty is slicing tomatoes. Two

cakes, one marked *chocolate* and one *vanilla*, rest in bakery boxes on the counter. I tell the twins happy birthday.

Bonnie looks up from her *Collective Apparitions* book. "Are you feeling better?" she asks me.

"I am."

"You don't look much better."

"Shut up."

"Bonnie is a wench and there's nothing to do about it," says Liberty. "But we're going tubing tomorrow morning if you want to come."

"Okay," I say.

"You can't drive. We're driving."

"Yeah."

Mummy gives me a hug, one of her long, concerned hugs, but I don't speak to her about anything.

Not yet. Not for a while, maybe.

Anyway, she knows I remember.

She knew when she came to my door, I could tell.

I let her give me a scone she's saved from breakfast and get myself some orange juice from the fridge.

I find a Sharpie and write on my hands.

Left: *Be a little.* Right: *Kinder.*

Outside, Taft and Will are goofing around in the Japanese garden. They are looking for unusual stones. I look with them. They tell me to search for glittery ones and also ones that could be arrowheads.

When Taft gives me a purple one he's found, because he remembers I like purple rocks, I put it in my pocket.

86

GRANDDAD AND I go to Edgartown that afternoon. Bess insists on driving us, but she goes off by herself while we go shopping. I find pretty fabric shoulder bags for the twins and Granddad insists on buying me a book of fairy tales at the Edgartown bookshop.

"I see Ed's back," I say as we wait at the register.

"Um-hm."

"You don't like him."

"Not that much."

"But he's here."

"Yes."

"With Carrie."

"Yes, he is." Granddad wrinkles his brow. "Now stop bothering me. Let's go to the fudge shop," he says. And so we do.

It is a good outing. He only calls me Mirren once.

THE BIRTHDAY IS celebrated at suppertime with cake and presents. Taft gets hopped up on sugar and scrapes his knee falling off a big rock in the garden. I take him into the bathroom to find a Band-Aid. "Mirren used to always do my Band-Aids," he tells me. "I mean, when I was little."

I squeeze his arm. "Do you want me to do your Band-Aids now?"

"Shut up," he says. "I'm ten already."

*   *   *

THE NEXT DAY I go to Cuddledown and look under the kitchen sink.

There are sponges there, and spray cleaner that smells like lemons. Paper towels. A jug of bleach.

I sweep away the crushed glass and tangled ribbons. I fill bags with empty bottles. I vacuum crushed potato chips. I scrub the sticky floor of the kitchen. Wash the quilts.

I wipe grime from windows and put the board games in the closet and clean the garbage from the bedrooms.

I leave the furniture as Mirren liked it.

On impulse, I take a pad of sketch paper and a ballpoint from Taft's room and begin to draw. They are barely more than stick figures, but you can tell they are my Liars.

Gat, with his dramatic nose, sits cross-legged, reading a book.

Mirren wears a bikini and dances.

Johnny sports a snorkeling mask and holds a crab in one hand.

When it's done, I stick the picture on the fridge next to the old crayon drawings of Dad, Gran, and the goldens.

87

ONCE UPON A time there was a king who had three beautiful daughters. These daughters grew to be women, and the women had children, beautiful children, so many, many children, only something bad happened,

something stupid,
criminal,
terrible,
something avoidable,
something that never should have happened,
and yet something that could, eventually, be forgiven.
The children died in a fire—all except one.
Only one was left, and she—
No, that's not right.
The children died in a fire, all except three girls and two *boys.*

There were three girls and two boys left.
Cadence, Liberty, Bonnie, Taft, and Will.

And the three princesses, the mothers, they crumbled in rage *and despair. They drank and shopped, starved and scrubbed* *and obsessed. They clung to one another in grief, forgave each* *other, and wept. The fathers raged, too, though they were far* *away; and the king, he descended into a delicate madness from* *which his old self only sometimes emerged.*

The children, they were crazy and sad. They were racked *with guilt for being alive, racked with pain in their heads and* *fear of ghosts, racked with nightmares and strange compulsions,* *punishments for being alive when the others were dead.*

The princesses, the fathers, the king, and the children, they *crumbled like eggshells, powdery and beautiful—for they were* *always beautiful. It seemed*
as if
as if
this tragedy marked the end of the family.
And perhaps it did.
But perhaps it did not.

They made a beautiful family. Still.

And they knew it. In fact, the mark of tragedy became, with time, a mark of glamour. A mark of mystery, and a source of fascination for those who viewed the family from afar.

"The eldest children died in a fire," they say, the villagers of Burlington, the neighbors in Cambridge, the private-school parents of lower Manhattan, and the senior citizens of Boston. "The island caught fire," they say. "Remember some summers ago?"

The three beautiful daughters became more beautiful still in the eyes of their beholders.

And this fact was not lost upon them. Nor upon their father, even in his decline.

Yet the remaining children,
Cadence, Liberty, Bonnie, Taft, and Will,
they know that tragedy is not glamorous.

They know it doesn't play out in life as it does on a stage or between the pages of a book. It is neither a punishment meted out nor a lesson conferred. Its horrors are not attributable to one single person.

Tragedy is ugly and tangled, stupid and confusing.
That is what the children know.
And they know that the stories
about their family
are both true and untrue.
There are endless variations.
And people will continue to tell them.

MY FULL NAME is Cadence Sinclair Eastman.

I live in Burlington, Vermont, with Mummy and three dogs.

I am nearly eighteen.

I own a well-used library card, an envelope full of dried beach roses, a book of fairy tales, and a handful of lovely purple rocks. Not much else.

I am
the perpetrator
of a foolish, deluded crime
that became
a tragedy.

Yes, it's true that I fell in love with someone and that he died, along with the two other people I loved best in this world. That has been the main thing to know about me,

the only thing about me for a very long time,
although I did not know it myself.
But there must be more to know.
There will be more.

MY FULL NAME is Cadence Sinclair Eastman.

I suffer migraines. I do not suffer fools.
I like a twist of meaning.
I endure.

ACKNOWLEDGMENTS

Thanks most of all to Beverly Horowitz and Elizabeth Kaplan for their support of this novel in countless ways. To Sarah Mlynowski (twice), Justine Larbalestier, Lauren Myracle, Scott Westerfeld, and Robin Wasserman for commenting on early drafts—I have never shown a manuscript to so many people and been in such dire need of each person's insights. Thanks to Sara Zarr, Ally Carter, and Len Jenkin as well.

Thanks to Libba Bray, Gayle Forman, Dan Poblacki, Sunita Apte, and Ayun Halliday, plus Robin, Sarah, and Bob for keeping me company and talking shop while I wrote this book. Gratitude to Donna Bray, Louisa Thompson, Eddie Gamarra, John Green, Melissa Sarver, and Arielle Datz. At Random House: Angela Carlino, Rebecca Gudelis, Lisa McClatchy, Colleen Fellingham, Alison Kolani, Rachel Feld, Adrienne Weintraub, Lisa Nadel, Judith Haut, Lauren Donovan, Dominique Cimina, and everyone who put so much creativity into helping this book find an audience.

Thanks especially to my family, who are nothing like the Sinclairs.

ABOUT THE AUTHOR

E. LOCKHART is the author of four books about Ruby Oliver: *The Boyfriend List, The Boy Book, The Treasure Map of Boys,* and *Real Live Boyfriends*. She also wrote *Fly on the Wall, Dramarama,* and *How to Be Bad* (the last with Sarah Mlynowski and Lauren Myracle). Her novel *The Disreputable History of Frankie Landau-Banks* was a Michael L. Printz Award Honor Book, a finalist for the National Book Award, and winner of a Cybils Award for Best Young Adult Novel. Visit E. online at emilylockhart.com and follow @elockhart on Twitter.